THE REVENGE PAWN

A SCOTTISH PSYCHOLOGICAL THRILLER

EMELLE ADAMS

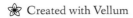

To Adam, Mum and Dave, Maria, John, Jack, Fiona and Daniel.
Thank you for listening to my mad plot lines, crazy theories on how to kill people, and for reading this in its raw form.

Rhiannon's Family Tree

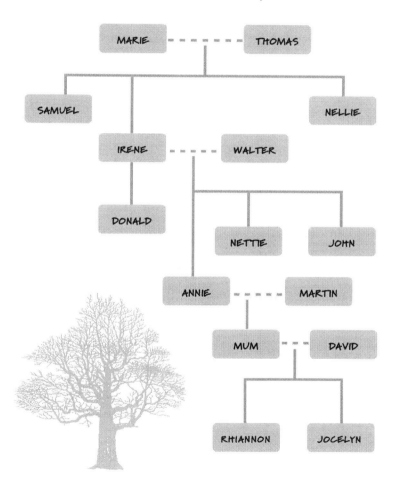

PART 1
THE OPENING

ONE

RHIANNON

I'M NOT SPOOKED or superstitious, living on the site of a murder. It occurred just before the first lockdown, over there, where the bookshelves now sit. The flat is sterile, a square box of a place with fancy fittings, but a box, nonetheless. Boxes have fewer shadows. Ghosts do not haunt modern flats.

I knew the guy who owned it before me—Preston. He lived in the village I grew up in. He was the chef at the pub where I worked over the summer holidays. I didn't know his brother, the victim. I'd forgotten he even had a brother until the murder became front-page news. Then I remembered his name, mentioned in hushed tones in the bar. I heard talk he'd been sent away.

The old folks from the village nodded in understanding when Preston's name cropped up, but no one elaborated on the murder. The brother had never shown up when I'd lived and worked there, but then, Preston was older than me. He must be in his sixties now, maybe even his seventies. You don't mix with folk fifteen or so years older than you when you're a young adult. After I moved away in my twenties, I didn't keep in contact. At that age, I never looked back.

TWO

RHIANNON

FORTUNATELY, the murder reduced the flat's asking price. I'd always considered that if I ever moved back to this area, these flats would be perfect—positioned near enough to the sea that I could smell the salt in the air, hear the cracking of boat sails and the clanking of ropes against masts in the distance. Seagulls squawked everywhere in the town, as they ventured inland to scavenge on the bins. Their screeching pleased me; it meant I was close to the shore. Conflated with COVID restrictions, the fear of buying houses without viewings (I knew the flat's layout, as my pal had lived in the next block), and the uncertainty of the times, the cost soon fell further to within my price range.

Not that I really thought I'd move back here. Then again, the cards I'd dealt out for myself did not involve Colin cheating on me either.

The events leading to my discovery of his infidelity were also a consequence of COVID lockdown. It's difficult to maintain an affair when your significant other is breathing down your neck 24/7. His opportunities to sneak and lie were snuffed out by spending all his time in the house with me. Both confined to working from home, I could not attend my amateur dramatic group's rehearsal, or gym, or meet up with pals. He couldn't participate in his supposed five-a-side football and golf. I noticed him disappearing with his phone into the toilet or chatting on the computer in the evening after home-working had finished. Work Zoom calls don't often happen after 10 pm. Not that I cared too much. I simply poured another wine, justifying it as not drinking alone, as he was in the building. Experts say that drinking two units of alcohol shortens your lifespan by nine minutes. Based on lockdown alone, I calculated I'd died around 1837.

Then he started hanging about in the shed, although the garden never appeared any different. I wanted all the D.I.Y. sorted. He had promised to do it for years, but it was never completed because he 'didn't have the time'. Suddenly gifted with time, still no work was finished.

It had been going on for about two years, the affair and the procrastinating about home improvements. He'd known her from university, before their Facebook friendship kicked off. Their shared past facilitated the flirtation, the fantasy, and then the reality.

They had met up on two to four occasions. Lies confused the details. His fake golf trips, his extended work conferences. 'These things just seem to happen,' he'd pleaded, as if chemistry and magic had taken over.

No, they didn't just happen, Colin. You chatted in private on purpose. You met up in a hotel lobby bar deliberately and intentionally booked a room!'

Small steps, like taking his credit card out of his wallet to pay for the hotel room, had occurred purposefully on his part. No third party or random event caused that. It was not a natural disaster; it was an unnatural one. A manmade catastrophe.

He bought me out of the house in the end. He could afford to, as she moved in to pay something towards the mortgage, with her name on there instead of mine—a rapid and royal replacement.

I hated the house by then, the place of so much deception, so I moved back near to where I'd grown up. Mum had packed up all her things and moved into the old folks' home there. She was at times lucid, at times vague, sometimes a shell. I could live close to her back in East Lothian, the forgotten county of Scotland—Edinburgh's embarrassing, common, less-educated wee sister.

Scotland's tourist brochures present only the castle and hill in Scotland's capital. That's what made the telly and the brochures. Growing up, if I heard East Lothian mentioned on the telly, I'd feel beyond excited. We existed! People in London realised we existed! Then I would cringe, embarrassed by my hometown's colloquial nature, hoping they wouldn't find out how old-fashioned we were, praying for the place to shrink back into obscurity.

THREE

RHIANNON

 I bought this notebook last week from a museum gift shop, and I'm writing in it almost daily.

I ventured out in lockdown number 'whatever' when some restrictions had been lifted and the museum, Abbey, and the shop reopened. I hadn't bought my ticket online. I thought I could turn up when I wanted, but I was refused entry.

I couldn't be bothered with the faff of ordering a ticket online outside the door, so I made a snap decision to walk away. I meandered around the wall and viewed the Abbey from there. I zoomed in with my phone and observed as well as the tourists over the perimeter wall did for their £13.95. This suited my Scottish meanness, but I still wanted to browse the shop at the end for something unnecessary.

Some of the Abbey and the courtyard and gardens were open to the public for free at the end. The sun shone, for a change, so I sat down on a bench for a while to enjoy my zero money's worth. On impulse, I jumped up and headed towards the door from the courtyard to the shop. It was the 'out door'. The official 'in door' was at the end of the museum, guiding you through the obligatory gift shop.

I nodded to the woman by the out door. With a suspicious air, she allowed me in. Of course, she did—I might spend money! But still, I perceived her wondering whether I might wander around the museum and Abbey in reverse and try to enter the attraction for free. I'd perhaps sneak in another 'out door'.

The door lady and the shop assistant behind the counter exchanged glances before Mrs. Door sauntered back to her job at the exit. The shop assistant, in turn, observed as I got perilously close to the door towards the attraction. I glanced at the name on her badge—Patsy. Patsy examined me, opened her mouth to say something, and then shut it again when I smiled and ambled back to the trinkets.

I disliked her staring at me. I've developed a fear of people. Since I've been on my own, people have become a threat, not an opportunity. I feel my lonesomeness more in company now than alone. I didn't want Patsy's eyes sliding over my skin, reading the discomfort in my shoulders and jaw.

In the flat, I was content in my solitude, but when I was in crowds, where couples gathered, I felt the worst. A woman on her own at a museum, without a man or even a woman, looks suspicious. I imagine them saying, 'What kind of person has no friends at all to meet up with? A museum is to be enjoyed together. What the hell is this weirdo doing roaming about alone?'

I didn't want Patsy talking to me or even offering to. I did not want her to extend an offer to join her in a conversational dance. I have forgotten how to speak.

My voice is a mumble or a squeak now. My sentences, a choked, alien noise. If I spoke, she might not understand. She might ask that I repeat every sentence two or three times, until I wished I had never spoken at all.

My chatter never stopped when I'd lived with Colin —perhaps he'd grown tired of that. He'd claimed I chirped like a budgie with fresh Trill, and more so with alcohol. Now, I don't produce words at all. I've been isolated for so long that I try speaking out loud at home and my voice echoes in the flat, haunting it like a memory.

What was I browsing touristy overpriced guff for anyway? A tartan scarf for twenty quid? A mug for twelve pounds? I have no money to fritter. The flat took all my cash, half the house's sale price.

I noticed a notebook with a chess piece on the front, with the word 'Queen' emblazoned across it. I felt drawn to the symbol of female power, when in real life I'm a pussy. I froze, feeling Patsy's gaze chill the back of my neck. Tension in my stomach rose with my anger up to my face.

Why is she picking on me? I thought. What move will I make next?

I stared at the notebook. The Queen never felt this nervous, I bet. I held it tight and read the quote on the back: The Queen possesses power and can move any direction, as long as there are no pieces in her way.

I proceeded at random, just to put Patsy on edge. Her stare followed me apprehensively as I made my move.

First, it appeared I was leaving; then, in a sudden shift, I turned back. She flinched and folded some scarves—the same one three times—and then sighed.

Distracted, she couldn't get it right. A man stood between us, wanting to be served, which startled Patsy, whose attention was fixed on me.

Giggling inside, I nipped behind a pillar and watched her in a mirror. When Patsy glanced up again, her eyes darted around the shop, trying to locate me. She locked the till and rushed to the museum's door to speak to Mrs. Door.

I made my move swiftly, appearing at the counter to pay, drumming my fingers impatiently. I tutted.

Colin used to say, 'Are you sucking a sweetie?' when I tutted.

I gripped the notebook with the Queen cover until Patsy rushed back and served me without comment. I carried the purchase out like a small prize.

Checkmate, Patsy!

FOUR

RHIANNON

 I've decided to write all my thoughts in this notebook with the Queen chess piece on the cover. I'm not certain of the purpose. Mum said journaling was a family tradition, although I don't remember seeing anyone ever actually doing it. I suppose I have no one to tell my thoughts to, no one like Colin to chirp on to. I have little else to do; there are no clubs open, no amateur drama to join in with. Everything is cancelled due to the virus. No social events or get-togethers are encouraged.

Some restrictions are lifting, but people are scared to start preparing an event that might need to be cancelled later. It would be a pain if all those 'am dram' rehearsals came to nothing. That happened last time. Two weeks before the show, Boris and Nicola came on the telly and told us all to stay in.

Moving here made me ponder whether I'd hallucinated my previous life or awoken from a dream. All of it played as a movie, detached from reality. It felt unreal, like someone else's life, or something I read in a book. It happened, however, and was not erased from history.

You cannot escape your past by moving to another postcode. The past is the past. Move on, leave it behind, I heard them say, whoever they are. But sometimes, it creeps up and sneaks into the present. It crawls into your future, despite any attempts to put it all behind you, and maps out what happens next. People have memories as long as you have. I forget that they will recall bits I have forgotten, parts I'd rather forget. Those parts could still pop up often in my mind and induce a physiological lurch in my stomach, a chemical jolt. Does the sympathetic nervous system cause that? (I never understood that at school. More like the unsympathetic nervous system.)

This isn't the first time I've left and then returned to this area. I attended university miles away. Four years later, I came back here for my first job. I encountered Kim again at my accountant's job in town. I'd known her all my life and even worked with her in the local bar over the summer holidays, but I'd forgotten all about her once I headed to university. There, I had another life; not in the village, something exciting. I'd filed Kim away in another section of my mind, along with the rest of my childhood and youth. I had been enjoying the present too much to consider those folks back there in Hicksville. But she wouldn't let me forget where I'd come from.

 My first job after university felt momentous. I had arrived at the interview early. When the owner came on the scene, I noticed him and decided I'd hang back, wait for him and the staff to enter, and then appear dead on time. He noticed me and shouted, 'Rhiannon?'

'Okay, here goes,' I whispered under my breath into my scarf and looked up. 'Yes, yes. It's me. I'm early. I can wait outside.'

'No, no. Come on in,' he said, struggling with the keys and the alarm. I stood as he turned on the lights. I felt uncomfortable, alone with a man in his forties when only in my twenties. Females often check the exits, create an escape plan. We are on guard when alone with a strange man, but maybe my nerves made me sense tension. His eyes scanned me up and down. Young and fit then, I was never drop-dead gorgeous. But youth is attractive, although I was not of that opinion at the time.

As we chatted and he showed me around, he realised I had grown up in this area, and that mattered—I know that now. People prefer the company of someone who speaks in the same manner as them. I didn't believe I had much chance at the interview, but the owner decided straight away. He never told me I'd got the job. He just asked, 'When can you start?'

'Right away!' I replied without missing a beat.

He nodded. 'Head down to see Kimberly and tell her you will be starting on Monday. She will sort you out with everything—your paperwork, keys, codes, and dress code, etcetera. See you Monday.' His eyes focused on his desk. It was my cue to leave. He had work to do.

'Okay. Amazing. Thanks.' I stood up, ruminating, Did that just happen? I'm living in the world of work and grown-ups now.

Delighted, I skipped down the stairs in a heady daze. My face must have been glowing. I stopped to breathe halfway down the stairs. Composing myself, I thought, Okay, let's find out about this dress code. Is there a uniform or something? Or a badge? And he mentioned keys ...

I headed through to the reception area and spotted three women gathered together. I approached the one who appeared the oldest. Sitting as the others stood, she gave the impression of being in charge.

'I'm looking for Kimberly?'

She glared and rolled her eyes at the girls, who giggled.

When she did not reply, I continued, 'I'm Rhiannon.' I said it with an inflexion that made it sound as if I doubted my own name.

'Yeah, I know,' she answered, peering at me with eyes up but her head down. After another pause, she added, 'I'm Kimberly.'

'Okay, right ... Kimberly.'

'Of course, I'm Kimberly. I've always been Kimberly,' she snapped, her head lifting again.

It seemed a strange turn of phrase. 'I've always been Kimberly.'

What did she mean? I struggled to comprehend, rattled by the frostiness in the air. I'd done something, said something wrong. I believe I'm quite clever, but I sometimes miss social subtleties—or the point.

I've always been Kimberly. I processed it again. I've always been Rhiannon. I ran both statements through in my brain. We'd all always been our name. At least I considered that true if you hadn't changed your name, of course. Maybe she believed I was suggesting she had once been Bonnie Prince Charlie in a previous life. I stood staring blankly for what seemed a long time, although I'm sure it only lasted seconds. Kimberly seemed irritated, annoyed even.

'Right. Okay, Kimberly.' I smiled—perhaps too

much—holding my drawn-on grin. Discomfort replaced the real joy I'd felt just moments earlier.

'Kim,' she huffed and folded her arms.

I blinked.

'Kim,' I repeated. A second later, I realised she was Kim, the same Kim I had known from the village and the bar.

'Oh yes—Kim! Silly me! Yes, I ... I didn't expect you in this context. When he said Kimberly, and you said Kimberly, it took me a minute. I didn't realise you worked here, and well ... sometimes my eyesight ...' I kept on, back-tracking and flubbing about, none of which caused her to back down.

She made me feel uncomfortable and carried on doing so. I'd forgotten her, and she would make me suffer for it. She couldn't help herself.

FIVE

RHIANNON

I SPEND DAYS EXISTING. I rise and dunk a single teabag in the cup. The teapots on show above the cupboards are never used; it's too much tea and effort. The fridge and the fruit bowl are never full. I can't eat all the fruit before it rots. My lot in the stores is individual portions, sad baskets of food—never a trolley. A man checks up on me every day and has done during most of this COVID thing. I look forward to his calls. He's from India and is very concerned about a car accident I can't recall. I stroll around town often. Town miles seem less boring than the country ones. I go to Mum's old house and sort through all the boxes, throwing out decades-old tax returns and papers.

I hike long distances until I'm in a trance: one step, then the other. I stride until all thoughts peter out, and all I'm left with is the sound of my breathing.

People who've lived here all along complain the place is not like it used to be. I left in their perfect past, so my memories aren't as nostalgic. When the Woolies shut, they were bereft. A Turkish barber's and an Argentinian restaurant augured the creeping multiculturalism of Edinburgh, the owners spreading out into East Lothian.

Perhaps the kebab shop folk moved here because they couldn't afford the cost of living in gentrified Edinburgh. Or perhaps they arrived at this part and thought, 'Oh look, they don't have a kebab shop.' The queues are huge, so they made a terrific choice.

In a packed box of Mum's in the old house, I found an old journal that belonged to my great-great-grandmother Marie, who also grew up here. I started reading it, but it's mostly family history or the usual village gossip. It made me think that if this place really has changed at all, it's probably for the best.

TODAY, I marched seven miles until I heard a familiar voice from a bench. This time, I recognised Kim straight away. She made an impression in those post-university years, more than she ever had on me as a child or youth. This time, I did not forget her.

I should pretend not to know her, I thought. *That would show she has no effect on me at all.*

But, of course, that's not what I did.

SIX

Notes

MARIE, 1897

THOMAS SPOKE to me despite his minister father's forbidding. I knew he waited for me around the village; he skulked, always. We weren't proper enough to speak to. We were rubbish—poor and Catholic. Father had moved here for work, further east than Glasgow, where he'd landed off the boat from Ireland.

The mines took him on in Lothian for less pay than other men, of course. They had whole pits for Catholics like us.

Thomas, Minnie, William, and I were all born on the same day: 15 June 1880. None of them was permitted to mix with me; they did, nonetheless.

They judged me Irish, although I never set foot in Ireland. We four, born in the shadow of Carberry, never comprehended how our lives would be connected.

Ma claimed all the boys would be attracted to me because I resembled her. She announced it with pity and exasperation.

'Why do Thomas and William follow me around?' I asked.

'No one can miss you. The height of you and those freckles. There's no doubting whose daughter you are.'

I snorted my reply.

'Don't laugh. It's a burden looking like this.'

'How, Ma?'

'Men's gaze on you all the time, and more than their gaze sometimes.' She drew a breath. 'You and I need a talk about those boys.'

FATHER HAD GIVEN her nine children, and on top of that, she carried coal at the top of the mine. Then she had bath night and visits to the Steamie in Smeaton to keep her busy. There, she heard the gossip before she trudged back with our clothes in the pram.

She never ran out of work. She prayed for rest and almost anticipated the permanent peace of death to deliver her from her labours.

Minnie, William, and Thomas attended school together at the primary school. Then, when they got older, the next school until they were twelve. I never bothered. Mother insisted I help her in the house with the younger ones. I couldn't have gone anyway. School was for the Protestants.

William left at twelve to work with his ploughman dad on the farm. He had the build—rugged, dark, strong, and sun-bronzed. He lived minutes from our house. I'd notice him lying in wait for me, like Thomas, but he never spoke much. Thomas spoke enough for the both of them.

One day, as I strode through the village, Thomas and William leant on a wall, staring as I marched past. They followed. Minnie, always around Thomas, joined in, toddling on behind.

'Hey, where are you going?' called Thomas. It was a Sunday, the day of rest. I had no business being in the house if I wanted rest. Instead, I walked for miles around the countryside, for hours at a time. I liked to march on and on until my mind felt freed, and my body exhausted. It made me strong and lean. I had control over that, at least.

'Walking,' I answered, not even glancing back.

'Where?' asked Thomas again. I shrugged, but I did not miss a step.

'Anywhere. I like walking.'

'I know where we can walk,' he replied. I didn't answer, but I stopped to spin and face them. I stood with my hands on my hips, my thumbs firm on the small of my back. Mother stood that way when facing up to father.

'You can't go with her, Thomas,' Minnie piped up. She had caught up and tugged his sleeve. She stood as close as she could at his side, scanning me up and down. The teacher's daughter, she considered Thomas, the minister's son, a perfect match for her. I was not as clean as her, but she didn't come close. Even with her fancy clothes, she was an unfortunate girl, squat and plain. I resembled my mother. A goddess in sackcloth.

'Why not?' Thomas shrugged Minnie off, without taking his eyes off me.

Minnie gave me a dismissive glance. 'You aren't to.'

'But you're here speaking to her, too.' He laughed at Minnie's screwed-up face.

William grunted. I glanced his way and smiled. He stood tall and handsome, his hair dark and curly. We all understood his background. His sister had brought him into the house, and no one knew his father. His Da probably wasn't his Da; his Ma not really his Ma. I didn't believe he realised. Everyone else had worked it out before he did. I heard they warned his sister not to bring any more children in, but she repeated the act, so at least he had one real brother.

William stepped forward, made to speak, and then gave up with nothing to say. Thomas, in contrast, never stopped talking. Tall and gangling with pointed features, Thomas had never done any work like William. William's hands were of a ploughman; Thomas had the hands of a gentlewoman.

I stopped and faced them.

'Follow on if you dare,' I challenged, turning to depart. Thomas followed.

'I'm telling,' Minnie called after him. William verged on joining in, but then he stalled. 'I ... I ... can't.' Strong in appearance but not in words, he couldn't force them out. He stared but did nothing.

'I'm coming. I love to walk. I'll show you places. Thomas trotted to match my pace. My long legs strode across the fields.

'Where?' I queried, not stopping or averting my gaze.

'Byre's Kirk.'

'Byre's Kirk, by Ormiston?' It was five miles from the village.

'Too far?' Thomas asked.

'No! I can walk that,' I snipped, striding on.

'You'll get in trouble,' shouted Minnie from afar. She didn't want Thomas disappearing off with me when it should have been her walking with him. She lumbered off dejectedly to tell whoever would listen.

WE MARCHED ON AND ON, up the hill to Carberry and the big house there. I liked walking for its own sake, but Thomas indicated he had something to show me. I hoped it wasn't what mother had warned me about, although I was curious. I felt safe with the slight, pale minister's son. Being stronger than him, I could fight him off. If it had been William, I might have thought differently.

Thomas led me into the woods. His strange demeanour gave me an upside-down feeling in my stomach. We were still in Carberry House grounds; it was a long trudge to Ormiston.

'This is where I've something to show you, and it's on the way anyway,' he announced.

We cut through some woodland, and Thomas halted. An enormous stone stood in front of us, isolated among the trees. The worn stone was engraved with a crown, letters, and numbers. I didn't know my letters or numbers, and Thomas knew it. Was he showing off? Mocking me?

When he was younger, he'd throw sticks and stones at me and run away, begging me to follow him. That stopped as he got older, when the lurking and staring began.

'You see it?' He hovered at my shoulder as I inspected it.

'So what?' I sniffed. I refused to be impressed by a stone with writing on it.

'I thought you'd like it.' He sounded disappointed.

I approached it. I stood on my tiptoes and followed two shapes with my fingers. He appeared behind me, holding my hand as we drew over them again together.

'Em. Ar,' he said.

He didn't seem to be mocking me. He seemed kind. His hands felt soft.

'Em. Ar,' I repeated. 'What's that mean?'

'M has the sound Em. And R has the sound Ar.'

'So, M and R,' I repeated in a whisper.

He gasped, 'Yes, MMMarie, RRRiordon—the letters from your name.'

'So, I'm Em Ar?' I raised my eyebrows in delight. He seemed pleased that I appreciated it. 'And a crown,' I noted.

'Yes. It's for Mary Regina.'

'Who's she then? I thought it was Marie Riordon.' I folded my arms in mock annoyance.

'Regina means queen. See the crown ... the crown there on the stone?' He held my hand and finger and marked it out again.

I stopped and eyed him square.

Thomas dropped his head and let my hand loose with a shrug. 'She was a queen.'

'A queen was here?' I questioned. It didn't seem likely. I scanned around, as if there might be proof, but all I saw was grass and trees.

'Mary Queen of Scots, the Queen of Scotland,' he explained.

I set about entwining twigs, Holly and birch. Thomas watched, bemused, until I placed them on my head. 'I am Marie Regina. I am the Queen of Scotland. Em Ar.'

He laughed and sat on the grass. I sat beside him.

'Thank you, I do like it,' I said.

He stared down again and toyed with a piece of grass.

'What does the rest of it say?'

'1567. At this spot, Mary...'

'I see Em and Ar again. Mmmmaaaarrrryy.' I showed off what a quick learner I could be.

'Queen of Scots...' Thomas paused as I fiddled with my crown and flicked my hair. I knew what I was doing. His mouth fell open. He closed it, cleared his throat. He continued. 'After the escape of Bothwell.'

'Who's he?' I butted in.

'The man she married.'

'He escaped? He left her? Here? Why did he not take her with him? Well, I don't think much of him!'

Thomas smiled and carried on reading.

'... she mounted her horse and surrendered to the confederate lords.'

'She surrendered? What's that all about?'

'She lost the confidence of her Lords.'

'Why?'

'Because of the man.'

I frowned. 'Typical'

'She married him after it was thought he had to do with the murder of her first man. Then folks believed she was to blame too.'

'She had a first man? She loved this new one, though, I bet. Daft woman, marrying one like that and getting all surrendered for him.

Him running off and escaping too. That's sad. Poor Mmmmmarrrry Rrrrregina... What's the last bit?'

'15 June 1567.'

'Same as our birthdays.'

'Yes, our birthdays.'

I cowed my head to the side.

Thomas swallowed so hard I almost heard it.

'What happened to her?'

'Taken to Edinburgh Castle, and then up to Loch Leven, and then she escaped.'

'Good!' I exclaimed. I stood up to examine the stone closer.

'Then was again captured at Langside.'

I sighed. I placed my hand on the stone and scanned the area, as if I might see her. I shut my eyes, and my bare feet felt the ground on which she had stood.

'She was taken in by her cousin Elizabeth, the Queen of England.'

'She was safe then?'

'No. Her cousin imprisoned her and chopped her head off,' he said matter-of-factly, as he strained to push himself up off the ground.

'No!' I exclaimed.

He howled with laughter, and then picked up a stick and knocked the head off some wildflowers. 'How don't you know this?' he asked.

'Why do I need to know this? I've to drag coal from the mine soon enough. I don't have to understand about queens and numbers and letters.'

He spoke quieter then. 'You don't need to do that. I'm for the university.' He attended the grammar school that no one in the area could afford but his family and Minnie's.

'What's that to do with me?' I questioned, realising what he meant.

He did not answer.

I laughed and gazed across the water as far as Fife. It seemed likely that the miner's daughter and the ploughman's son should get together. We'd produce handsome children, all poor forever. The teacher's daughter and the minister's son would be ideal.

Yet here we stood, him and me together, with Thomas hinting at a decision I could make to change that perfect plan.

SEVEN

RHIANNON

'HIYA,' pipes up the voice from the bench. It sounds like an 'I've caught you' type of opening.

'Oh, hi! Kim!' I shout, my shock evident. She pauses and peers down her nose at me from a sitting position. How could she do that?

'How are you?' I ask, breaking the silence.

'Fine.' She is unchanged. The years have been less kind to me. I'm scrawny not slender now. During one spat, the woman Colin replaced me with said I had more wrinkles than a glue sniffer's bag.

'How are you? What are you doing back? Visiting? Been up to the village?' She fires questions at me with a smirk. My heart beats faster. I need to decide what to say, because she always puts me on edge.

I get a grip. *We're older now, so surely I'm being silly,* I think, babbling, 'No, not been in a while to the village, most of the family have died now. Mum lives in the home along ...' I point in the general direction of the home, but its name escapes me. 'So yeah, I'm back here. In town, though—not the village. I've moved back.'

She says nothing, so I prattle on. 'Got a job at the accountants across town.'

The swanky place I work at on the far side of town is an improvement on that first job; no one knows me from my past there.

'It's great. I like it there, and it's comforting to be home, and ...'

Kim smiles, pauses, and takes a bite of her sandwich.

After a hellish long silence while she chews and then swallows, all the time not taking her eyes off me, she says, 'Traitor.'

She stabs me with one word before giving a huge toothy grin. Kim possesses a way of grinning so that all of her bottom teeth are visible, as well as the top ones. The appearance verges on a grimace. I feel myself heat up and redden. Not knowing what to say, I stand there gaping like a forgotten fish won at a fairground, whose bowl of water has not been changed since the novelty wore off.

She cackles at my open mouth. How the hell can she seem so friendly to begin with, but then deliver a piercing stab from a virtual verbal knife, with a smile at the end. I thought time had passed enough for her to be over me. Unfortunately, the local smiling assassin remembers me after all those years. As the victor, she should have forgotten me. Instead, she took another jab. At least I made some impact on her, but her reaction makes my stomach tighten with the fear she might come after me again.

I'm not paranoid; she was always out to get me.

'Oh, well, maybe see you around,' she mutters, standing and brushing non-existent crumbs from her perfect blue suit and black-and-white checked scarf. I watch as she crosses the road back to the building we had worked in together all those years before. She got rid of me there, as she wanted, and she has stayed in her position the entire time. A job for life, not three miles from where she grew up.

Kim marches, upright with her head held high, across the road and does not look back. She grips her lunch box by its tiny handle, her arm straight and certain. I'd recognise her a mile away from her posture, even from the back.

Jesus wept, I think, as I stumble home, telling myself over and over to forget all about her.

'Stupid woman is bloody mental,' I mutter, as I cross the bridge.

A born bully. She bullied in the village, in the shop, when I worked with her in the bar, and at the accountant's office. She consistently behaved that way throughout her life. For some reason, she couldn't leave me alone.

Unable to cope with Kim's bullying, when I worked with her after university, I decided to disappear forever, or so I thought. I could only take so much.

Work takes up so much time there is little left for anything else. It took too much of my existence to suffer that tight feeling in my chest five days a week from 9 to 5. I decided to work where no one knew my background, so they wouldn't judge me for 'getting above my station' as Kim did.

I won't be 'jumped up', as Kim claims I am. I'll be the qualified person I am, my younger self thought. Impostor syndrome stopped that plan from coming to fruition; also, my accent didn't help.

People with a proper accent sound clever. The number of times I've been mistaken for the secretary or the cleaner—I've lost count. To begin with, I'd blamed my youth and being female. I ruled out youth as I aged and still noticed the judgment.

'You don't look like an accountant.'

I put on a posher voice, dressed smarter, but what else?

How I hold myself?

If I'd possessed Kim's posture, maybe they'd think me more deserving.

EIGHT

RHIANNON

 My first week back, and I had her to deal with all over again. Bloody bitch!

I felt physically sick and dizzy all day. She's made me ill already. I read that boffins are saying queasiness and loss of balance are new COVID-19 symptoms. Maybe it's finally got me. My second wine delivery this week arrived, and I realised I now know the delivery guy by his first name. I checked my bank statement. Yeah, COVID caused me to lose my balance, all right.

Earlier today, I found myself in an Aldi supermarket. It mainly sells food but has a random item section of anything from sports socks to xylophones. The shelves were almost bare of food. The toilet roll frenzy was over, but now there's not enough lorry drivers to deliver the goods. They were down to their last few egg-timers and pieces of scuba gear. I found myself in the only aisle I'll ever walk down—the wine aisle—and picked up another bottle for no reason at all. I grabbed a random coconut, too, since they were on sale, and headed home. After breaking into the box of wine, I cried for all the times she hurt me. Thousands of people in this town, and she still found me. I shouldn't have come back.

I haven't cried since the break-up, and then not as much and not as loud as today. Crying alone in the flat is hopeless; the noise sounds so hollow with no one to sympathise. What is it for? Who is it for?

I sobbed until I ran out of energy and washed my face and decided to forget all about her and read great-great-great Granny Marie's journal for a while instead.

What is the point of thinking about Kim, after all? I need to work, live my life, leave it all in the past. Just thank God for my flat, my job and the fact I do not work with that bitch anymore.

NINE

Notes

MARIE, 1897

WE STRODE on to Byre's Kirk with scant words spoken. When I walked on my own, I marched on in silence, appreciating the benefit of the stride, the crisp air deep in my lungs, the clearness in my head. The habit was hard to break, even with company. Too much conversation slowed me down.

'Robert Burns's sister laid a headstone here,' Thomas announced when we arrived at Byre's Kirk graveyard.

'I've heard of him,' I replied.

Thomas stood on a fallen stone and announced:

> *'O my Luve is like a red, red rose*
> *That's newly sprung in June;*
> *O my Luve is like the melody*
> *That's sweetly played in tune.*
> *So fair art thou, my bonnie lass,*
> *So deep in luve am I;*
> *And I will luve thee still, my dear,*

Till a' the seas gang dry.'

'What?' I stood with my thumbs in my back and tried to look unimpressed. He made me smile, though.

'Burns.' He shrugged and stared at the ground, kicking a stone with his shoe. 'It's not the original church,' he continued, staring up at me. 'This is quite new. Forty or so years old, but there's been a church here since the 1600s.'

'You talk funny,' I mumbled, sauntering out of the graveyard to head back to the village.

Thomas gestured for me to continue.

'It's getting dark soon.' I shook my head.

'One more thing.'

I followed, curious and reckless as usual.

He took me on to a great house, and then past it. I spied a large wall of a bush—no, a tree, of dark green. He led me by the hand under the branches, which formed a tunnel that opened into an enormous cathedral-like space supported by two tree trunks. I touched one of the ten-foot-wide trunks and stroked the gnarled, entwined and contorted branches. The tree's crooked limbs flowed like scaly tendrils to the forest floor, creating a canopy above a magical secret room.

I gasped.

'I never knew this was here. What is this place?' I whispered. It seemed too holy to speak otherwise.

'We're in the Earl of Hopetoun's Garden. The house, Ormiston Hall, was built for the Cockburns, but they fell on hard times and sold it to Hopetoun. This,' he announced, slapping the trunk, 'is the Ormiston yew. It's a very sacred place.'

I spun around, covered by the largest tree I'd ever seen. Its boughs rose and fell around me. Giant, distorted antlers of branches reached hundreds of ways, with several trunks resembling arms with tortured sinews, while others lay dead straight. Some patches of wood appeared smooth as liquid, other parts, spiny.

'It's ancient. Druids held the yew tree sacred in pre-Christian times. The branches can root and form new trunks where they touch the ground, so yew trees symbolise death and resurrection for the Celts.'

'As old as Mary Regina?' I asked

'Older.'

'Older!'

'Although around the time of Mary. Some say John Knox preached here, but that's not right. He never did. He met a man named George Wishart, who did.'

'Who is John Knox?' I queried, still in the centre of the canopy.

'A protestant minister. He didn't like Mary Queen of Scots.'

'Why?'

'She was Catholic.'

I swivelled from surveying the roof of this forest church. 'Well, I don't like him.'

Thomas laughed with delight and continued. 'There's a poem about this tree.'

I let him continue.

> 'Beneath thy dark umbrageous shade
> The village swain delights to rove,
> To tell his kind-consenting maid,
> The soft voluptuous tale of love;
> While blushes tinge her rosy cheeks,
> As crimson rays o'er snow-wreaths steal,
> The silent sigh too well bespeaks
> What maiden lips may not reveal.'

Thomas came close. I felt his soft hands in mine, his warm breath.

'I'm Catholic,' I announced straight at him.

He shifted his feet and hesitated. 'Change—for me. You'll never want.'

I made a decision to write my own script.

ALL FOUR OF us married in the same month in 1898. William and Minnie had to settle for each other, since I chose Thomas. Minnie had to marry, I believed, although she said the same about me. Anyone with common sense could work out the dates. She hated me from then; she always hated me.

I changed my religion from the Catholic of Mary Queen of Scots to the Protestant of John Knox. My parents never spoke to me after that day. They surmised that I considered myself better than them.

I left Ma with the rest of her brood.

I had made my decision to escape, but I didn't know it would also be my imprisonment.

TEN

RHIANNON

 Yesterday, I fell asleep on the couch in the middle of the day and woke up bewildered. For a few seconds, I wondered where I was. It wasn't the ceiling I banked on. It was like I'd time-travelled for a moment. I expected to recognise a bumpy, cracked area with cornice that needed dusting. I never cleaned right into all the bumps and grooves, which had been painted so many times they'd lost all definition. There should have been a couple of cobwebs I meant to deal with, too. I never got to those either.

I shook my head, rubbed my eyes and jolted into the present, staring at the smooth, modern lines of the flat I now lived in. Then I remembered that that was then, and this was now. My new normal. No longer masks and sanitising hands—the present. My now. This murder flat.

Occasionally, I drifted off until I was back living in the house that Colin and I had shared. Then, of course, sometimes I returned to the terraced house where I spent my youth. The somnolent brain doesn't recognise time; my neurons repeatedly send familiar signals by the same well-trodden pathways.

A bloody murder took place in this very room, but I didn't see any sign of it. The victim had his throat slit one year ago today. Right there too! I felt nothing.

Perhaps that's what I should have been dreaming about: something sinister, some sadness, repulsion—any emotion that could comprehend what occurred. However, it was an ordinary sunny day. The living rooms faced south, and the sun shone in, giving the room an upbeat appearance. Didn't the sun know not to shine on the site of a killing?

I searched for a clue: a blood stain, a mark on the skirting board. I don't know what I expected. The benefit of living alone is being able to crawl around your living area without having to explain yourself.

The neighbour from the flat above, Angela, had murdered the guy due to madness, illness, and a grudge from years ago. I had known Angela: a quiet, sensible girl. I'd curled my lip and shuddered at the idea she had cold-bloodedly slit a man's throat. It seemed unreal. But they'd convicted her, locked her up. I heard she was dying in a hospice now, though, released on compassionate grounds.

On my hands and knees, I kept looking, finally finding a feather jammed between the skirting and the carpet. Few birds possess pink feathers, unless Preston owned a parrot or a flamingo. I guessed it had come from a feather boa or fancy hat. I knew Preston well enough to conclude it was the boa option, which was confirmed when I found glitter too. I was so close to the floor that I could feel the carpet rough on one side of my face and the heat of sunlight on the other.

Glitter never leaves. Even if they ripped up the crime-scene carpets, glitter would work its way onto the new floor covering. I once heard a mother call it the devil's sand. The glitter could have come from Preston, or from the person before him; it's so persistent. I lay with my head on the floor, staring at the shimmer while the sun warmed my cheek. I left the glitter there. It would be impossible to get rid of anyway, like stains—or the past.

I say I knew Angela, but I mean that we attended the same fee-paying girls' high school in Edinburgh. At home time, we caught the bus together to the town where they lived, and I'd continue on to the village 2 miles away. I only moved to the town later, so we had different primary schools up to the age of 10. I was in her wee sister's class, so I was just friends enough to say hello. To me, boring, chubby tomboy Angela existed to take care of her sister, Alyssa. They joined our high school about the same time I started there. Angela's parents put her there due to bullying by the famously mad Tracey—that nutter was never out the court pages, although Angela stole her headlines with the throat-cutting.

I had gained a scholarship for kids from working-class backgrounds. I never spent time with Angela out of school, nor did I see Alyssa much. I believe Angela moved away for a while, but Alyssa still lives nearby with her rich husband, although she has kept her head down since the trial and all the media attention.

Preston had tried to help Angela hide the body, wrapped in bin bags in the communal bins, but the neighbour's son, Magnus, had clocked them. He called the police and reported that he witnessed his neighbours acting strangely in the dead of night.

He's one to talk! He's a funny one himself. His light

flickers on and off at all hours. Pale skin, greasy hair; he strikes me as a gamer. He can chat to friends around the globe but can't look someone in the next block in the eye.

I can't imagine Preston being involved, so I never understood why it took place in his flat, although the victim was his brother. If he'd called the police right away, he wouldn't have got into trouble.

I never did find out why he helped her try to cover it up. Perhaps he was afraid.

ELEVEN

Notes

MARIE, 1913

MINNIE HAD MARRIED BENEATH HERSELF. I felt her misery: the way she sneered at everyone or solely at me. She'd had an identical scowl when we were young, permanently on her face. Even on her wedding day, she'd had that curl to her lip. I knew William still leered at me; they all did.

Minnie wouldn't even share the shop with me in the village if she could avoid it. The women around here never took to me, all because of my background. What I'd have done to change places with angry, bitter Minnie, though.

I strode out still, of course—miles and miles. They'd say it was unseemly. I felt their scorn, but at least I lived comfortably. William worked from dawn until sunset, and still Minnie needed to pick tatties to earn extra money. I wondered what he was like. He wouldn't be talking and being clever all the time like Thomas.

'Did you know this?' he'd say, and 'Did you know that?' He knew full well I knew nothing.

WHEN THOMAS'S FATHER DIED, we received a share of his money. Of course, his older brothers had their share too, so there wasn't as much as expected. Still, I didn't need to haul coal and pick tatties. But I'd made my bed, and I lay in it. Then Minnie crossed my mind, her face sneering, lying in William's arms.

I headed to the main town to shop; there was more choice down the hill, by the sea. I loved the clamour of the fishwives shouting and calling. I felt the freshness in the air and breathed in the biting salt. Maybe my ancestors had sailed the sea as marauding seafarers or pirates. I joined the queue at the shop. Minnie stood in front of me, two down. She glanced back and then turned away with a sniff.

Leaning forward, I whispered over her shoulder, 'Can you tell your Johnny to leave Irene alone?'

'No idea what you mean?' she replied with the slightest turn of her head.

'Throwing stones at her and chasing.' I went on.

She considered that for a second. 'More the other way about.'

'Not one bit,' I snipped.

'Like her mother,' Minnie snapped.

The woman between us raised her eyebrows and dared turn to see who bit at the back end of this conversation.

'What do you mean by that?' I continued.

'You know fine.'

'I don't!'

'Fine you do.'

The woman between us heard it all and giggled.

Minnie headed out.

After paying, I found her outside waiting, talking to the woman who had been directly behind her in the queue. They quietened as I strolled past.

She followed me with her friend, scuttling to keep up. We continued to the river and the bridge.

'You think you are special.'

I ignored her.

'We all know what you are,' she goaded.

I stopped.

'That first one of yours is a bastard.' She told her own truth there, but she had gone too far.

I turned and grabbed her hair, yanking it until she stumbled in the dirt. People had followed from the shop to watch the show. Her friend picked her up.

'I told you what she was like.' Minnie got up and inhaled deeply before continuing. I slapped her hard in the face and left her with the gasps of the onlookers. Striding on, I marched barefoot for miles in the wrong direction. I understood what I was, all right, and where I came from. The daughter of an Irish miner. The great-great-granddaughter of a pirate.

I RETURNED HOME to muffled voices in the drawing room.

'Of course, Minnie. I understand.' Thomas consoled her.

'Well, I thought you should know. It's the talk of the town.'

The door creaked as I opened it. She brushed past me as if she owned the place.

I gave her a dry glare.

'You cannot behave like that. You must conduct yourself properly, woman. You are a minister's wife. How can I show my face and tell people right from wrong when you are rolling in the dirt?'

'I'll think you'll find it was Minnie in the dirt.'

'Where are your shoes?'

Miss Prim could do no wrong, and she had dished her story out ahead of mine. The first to tell the story is always believed; the other side seems a defensive explanation.

'You were behaving like a pair of fishwives.'

'You accept she was to blame?'

'Both of you! But I believe you were the start of this. Don't you feel sorry for poor Minnie—she with that boor William?'

'Nothing wrong with William,' I ventured.

'No? Well, maybe you should have married the ploughman. A brawling fishwife would have been a more befitting wife for him. I can't even look at you now.' He gestured for me to leave.

I stormed out.

He didn't want me. Him? Him with his soft hands and his talk. He'd wanted me all along, but now he had me, I wasn't enough. Tears of rage streaked my face.

I SPOTTED Minnie hanging around staring at the house, gloating at her win. She spied me and turned down the river path. I followed to the river. She started to run, but I was always faster than her, with my long legs.

We fought again, pulling hair and shoving until I pushed her in the water. The river flowed fast, and she floated towards the weir, gasping and dipping under. I didn't realise she couldn't swim until she began flailing about. For a second, I knew I could have left her to drown, but I ran to the top of the weir, waded in and caught her. I dragged her out and set her, coughing, on the bank.

I sprawled beside her, puffed.

'You nearly killed me, you animal,' she spluttered.

'But I didn't. I'll not hang for you, Minnie.'

We both lay there, wet and exhausted, for minutes before I began to laugh—hard.

She pulled herself up. 'You're not right, Marie. A witch.'

'They used to throw witches in the water to see whether they drowned or not, Minnie. And look at that ... you survived. So ... who's the witch?'

TWELVE

RHIANNON

 I'd felt mentally disconnected from Colin for years anyway. He couldn't be bothered with me by the end, by which time I had stopped caring that he wasn't bothered. I felt content only in the habit.

Our commitment was cemented by collective property ownership ... until he fell in love with her. Then he became addicted to that feeling of falling. He's had another two women since, each younger than the last.

Our relationship started well, or it wouldn't have continued, I guess. Relationships always start well. Everyone acts on their best behaviour. Everyone seems nice at the beginning, when they're trying to make you love them. I suggested that to someone, who seemed upset, even disgusted, with me. 'What do you mean? Are you pretending to be someone else?'

Now, I keep that opinion to myself.

I don't mean lying. I mean not revealing all your bad habits. Initially, romantic love makes you want to appear to be the best person, not to fool another you are perfect. All your bad habits and moods are shoved aside, but they soon creep back into the light from the dark insides of your gut. Then, the new lovers find things—or even search for things—to hate about each other. The criticisms, the complaints, the resentments build up until all that is left is disdain, never mind that it all started with such promise.

A fresh start feels similar to a new relationship; all seems well until the real you and the past catch up. There is no escaping it.

Children never came; Colin claimed we weren't ready for that. Now, I believe that maybe they would have put a lock on the relationship. We weren't married, so there was no ball and chain. It was easy to escape. The door was always open, so no one could get hurt ... apart from me.

The years carried on, and now a middle-aged me sits alone, and him with the latest one, just thirty-three years old, pregnant. Not even the sixty-year-olds consider me as a mate now. All the oldies want a thirty-three-year-old, too. That's the maximum age limit for them. I'm over it.

I didn't love him at the end, but somehow, I miss him. Maybe I miss another person being in the building. Perhaps I'll tape that coconut I bought on impulse to a mop, prop it up in the corner and not notice the difference. Actually, it might be an upgrade on Colin.

I prefer the daytime. I hear thumps and bumps, and now and then, some human life. Even the man who comes to clean the stairs gives me comfort, bashing around. I withdrew from life while I was in the relationship, and by the time I stopped wanting to withdraw, it was too late. I'd painted myself into a corner. I'd felt so safe and secure that I didn't try to build connections and neglected the ones I'd had. I moved away emotionally, then physically as well.

Now, I'm more withdrawn than I have ever been. I don't want to let my guard down and allow folks to notice any weaknesses they can hate. They'll certainly find something about me to dislike.

People enjoy picking apart others, even when they're worse themselves. One friend sat in my pretty clean house and delighted in pointing out a twisted phone cable or a stained cushion. Two flaws in the house, and she spotted them immediately.

I try to never let myself be bullied—well, not as much—but I'm too much of a people pleaser. I try to seem lovely, yet I don't trust anyone described to me as lovely. They probably aren't. They're probably trying to get what they can from you. They'll probably manipulate you into doing them favours.

THIRTEEN

Notes

MARIE

I wasn't sorry when Minnie died. After the incident, she'd dragged herself home but took ill with a fever. Her breathing never recovered entirely. I'd nearly drowned her, not knowing she was four months pregnant.

She weakened, and when the birth proved a difficult one, she struggled and couldn't survive it. She called on me when having the bairn, and I let her die to save the child. I felt nothing.

No one questioned her dying. She had clearly suffered throughout her confinement, and, perhaps out of shame, I was certain she had never told anyone that I had thrown her in the river.

William and Minnie had a brood of four before James, the final one, was born in 1906. By then, I was twenty-five and six children in. Until her death, Minnie and I had carried on with our mirrored lives: our firstborn the same year (Samuel for me, and Johnny for her), and then a child a year, and two lost in infancy to scarlet fever.

It's my fault Minnie's children have no mother and a father who can't bring them up. I felt sorry for the children she left behind—and for William. I didn't know how I felt about him. He had a heavy sadness about him. I'd never believed he thought much of her, but those children must be a burden to bear. He drinks now, but no one can fault him for that, not with all of his troubles.

I watched William at the funeral Thomas conducted for Minnie. No expression lit his face, but his eyes fell on me and lingered.

Thomas could hardly stammer the words for the wife he should have taken: the one who would not have embarrassed him. Minnie had wanted Thomas, but I wouldn't let her take my rescue—my way out of stinking poverty, of floors packed down with dirt. I walked on floorboards and rugs in the manse.

But living at the manse while Thomas attended university felt like mere existence. I wasn't free. I had hours of study to learn to read and write letters befitting a minister's wife. Sewing, and then babies born thick and fast, as he could not leave me alone despite never spending long on the act itself. I once heard Mother say she wished the business over quicker; Father wouldn't leave her alone at all either.

As a minister's wife, my position included visiting the widows, widowers, and needy. Now, William needed me, but not in the way the others had. The day after the mining disaster, I found out my father had suffocated underground. I was in the shop, buying a food parcel for William, when I heard my father had perished. I never believed I would feel grief, but a helpless need and sadness welled inside me. I could have lain down flat, facedown in the dirt, to ease the weight on my chest. I stumbled on, thinking how Father had lived and died underground.

Still, having promised to visit William, I kept my promise. I made it to William's with the food, although I couldn't remember getting there. I visited in silence. He never spoke much, but he uttered one sentence: 'I heard about your father.'

When he held me close, I never felt so loved. What followed seemed natural. Inevitable. Detached from all conscious thought. All I recall, even now, is staring at the lit Tilley lamp as we lay down in the box bed. When I returned home, Thomas was already asleep on the chair, the paper open at the news of the deaths. When he woke, he never spoke of it. He never mentioned my father.

THAT YEAR, I had a dark, curly-haired child—Francis. I passed his appearance off. All my family back in Ireland looked identical. 'All had that appearance in Donegal,' I maintained. 'Dark curly hair, blue eyes, every one of them.'

Thomas understood. He had married for lust. He preached about it in church, catching my eye. But then, in the dark, he couldn't fight it. Still, it happened less and less, at least. He wanted me, but things had changed in how he lay with me. No gentle, tender-handed Thomas came to bed, but a rough, angry one. More bairns were born, none of them with Francis's colouring. Maybe he knew.

Fourteen years of one child a year, until I was thirty-three. Thomas would still come to me, now and then, but he hated me for all I was: dirty, Irish, barefoot. A temptation. A sin. He resented me for all of it.

At Christmas 1913, I sensed another child growing in me. Rumours swirled of war, but they always did. I wondered what the next year would bring. War might come, but I was not worried. My children were too young to fight. Samuel, my eldest, was just fourteen. If war came, he would be just a bairn, and wars never lasted long.

FOURTEEN
RHIANNON

SCROLLING on my phone in bed, I see a comedian telling a joke about one-night stands.

'I don't have one night stands. I have two: one either side of my bed.'

I giggle and then sigh.

The Internet makes me feel less alone but still lonely at the same time. I keep it on until I am almost asleep, keeping the silence at bay. I hate turning the noise off to the quiet, heavy darkness. It rings in my ears, and I hear my own breathing. I don't want the pain of the stillness while I'm more than half awake.

I know I am ready for solitude when I experience a feeling similar to that first draw of nitrous oxide during dental treatment. I float ... aware of the drifting. I am ready for the seclusion, the seduction of sleep. But if that is interrupted, I lie awake, and the thinking starts. I lie in bed, pondering everything, from when I returned here (and why!) to that first job with Kim, and the only solution then is to get up and read Granny Marie's journal or write something or get online again.

I tried establishing myself here, but some people who knew me growing up wouldn't let me. I'd hang out with folks from the village, but they couldn't cope with me being a professional. I was Rhiannon from the Crescent. I was 'her what went to that posh school' and not the local grammar, as Kim had. I'd heard her snarl one day, 'If I'd gone to that posh school, I could have been an accountant too.'

All in all, I tried to become a person with a professional status, but the usual condemnation for considering myself 'better' remained. I was 'one of that lot' who disappeared away for a while and then came back. If they had been off living a life somewhere else, with different people, they wouldn't have remembered me at all, but this place was their whole life.

What do I remember about growing up here? When you are older, you are conscious. You remember to take photos, write a journal, or muse *I'll remember this*. But when you are young, you live without noticing. There's no deliberate awareness, no mindfulness. You exist. You rely on electrical impulses, triggers in your brain getting tapped again later.

I recall that I once fell over and ended up with a black eye on the day the photographer visited for our official photos, as we didn't own a camera. I know Mum still has the photo.

I remember picking tatties in the fields, the taste of freshly picked tatties with egg.

I remember that visits to the village became stranger in my teenage years. We had moved to the town by then, and my eyes were open to a modern world. The village always had a nod to the past.

My great-granny Irene, in her pinny, seemed to come from a different century, never mind another decade. In the eighties, I owned a Walkman, and she, a scrubbing brush. My family there did not seem sophisticated, or aware of cultural change. I felt uncomfortable, even in granny's house. My frail great-great grandmother Marie, who was over a hundred, and great-grandmother Irene lived in the village together. I remember the coal fire and the sideboard full of sweets. Decorated in 1950s colours, it seemed unlike the houses of my peers.

I'd sit on a hard chair brought in from the kitchen table, as the armchairs and couch were full. It was not called a couch at school; it was a sofa. The living room was now the lounge or drawing room; even the words seemed different.

I learned to change what I called things depending on where I found myself. The extra chairs from the kitchen table all sat at a different height, so I was perched up higher up than the adults. On the kitchen table, there was no milk jug or butter dish. They took them straight from the containers. Great-granny Irene made clootie dumpling wrapped in a rag. I remember I was able to tolerate that, for all my snobbishness.

When I attended the private school, my family was immediately suspicious of me. My Granny Annie, also now living in the town, saw some kid being held by their feet out of the Grammar School window and decided I wouldn't attend there.

I passed the exam for entry on a scholarship for poor kids to attend the posh, private girls' school up town. At the end of term, I'd come off the bus, wearing my green uniform and carrying my lacrosse stick and all my bags, and run the gauntlet of the village kids. I felt lucky to escape with chewing gum in my red hair and spit on my back from Kimberly and her pals.

I was an outsider, as Granny Marie had told me she once was. I never fitted in. Eventually, we learned to all lumber off the bus together, laden with our art projects, sports kits and sewing for the term. There was safety in numbers: Angela, a bit older, and her sister Alyssa, and me with my wee sister Jocelyn in tow, younger still.

I noticed Kim hanging on the corner with a gang of youths. She must have been nearly eighteen by then; some of her friends were older, some younger. They were waiting for the bus back to the village. Tension followed us into the park as we headed toward home.

'Ginger!' Someone shouted.

'Snobs,' another called.

Then another stood in our way.

'What's with the green uniforms, then? What school is this,

then?' One of them flicked the badge on Jocelyn's jacket. They always picked on the smallest one first.

Alyssa, so innocent and, frankly, a bit stupid, happily announced, 'St Margaret's!'

Angela groaned. 'Keep walking,' she said, as we pushed past them.

'What's wrong? We no' good enough to speak to?' The first bully yelled after us.

I grabbed Jocelyn as she spun to speak to them, but Angela did not catch Alyssa quick enough.

'No.'

She clearly meant they *were* good enough to speak to, but they took it the other way.

'Papes.'

'What?' questioned Alyssa.

Angela, sensing danger, shouted, 'Run!'

We ran into the park, followed by a mob of them. We sheltered behind a bench while they showered us from across the path with anything they could find.

'What's happening?' cried Alyssa.

'They hate us,' said Angela.

'Why?'

'They think we are snobs.'

'And Catholics, cos we wear green, and the school is St something,' I added. 'They don't like Catholics.'

'What's a Catholic?' said Alyssa, as a clod of earth flew over our heads.

I held up my lacrosse stick to protect myself.

'You know, the religion.' Jocelyn was younger than Alyssa but had miles more sense. 'Me and Rhiannon are Catholics, but you and Angela aren't.'

'What're we then?'

'Protestants, like them,' hissed Angela.

'Well, they shouldn't be chasing us then,' Alyssa declared, getting up from behind the bench. The throwing diminished, but a stone caught her on the shoulder. We watched in disbelief as she stood on the bench, arms wide open and shouted, 'Stop! Stop! There's been a mistake. It's all right. We're not Catholics. We are prostitutes!'

As we ran for our lives from Kimberly and her mob, Angela turned to her daft, wee sister and shouted, 'You just made that a whole lot worse!'

THEY NEVER FORGOT. Kim never forgot. She remembers everything. I filed away this part of my life in my memory cabinet. But now, I'm opening it all up. It's all flooding back. I'll remember all the details about it and about her. I'll make certain of it.

Every. Single. Damn. Thing.

FIFTEEN

Notes

MARIE, 1918

I WAS CORRECT; I was expecting, but I was not the only one. In the spring of 1914, Irene, aged fourteen, travelled to my cousins in the west. I made out she had moved to help my family there, who were in need. It made sense. Everyone knew they were poor Irish immigrants with too many children—of course they'd have nothing. Irene was a strong girl but not bright at school and not destined for the university like the boys. On 4 August, the war I never believed would happen began, and Irene gave birth to her firstborn, Donald. Thomas refused to speak to her. For years, he looked at her in the same disgusted way he judged me after Francis.

I didn't know who the father was, and she wouldn't tell me. I thought it could be Johnny, Minnie's boy, who was friends with Samuel. She shouted that it wasn't him so forcefully that I believed her. She maintained she would never tell me.

I had Nellie, my bairn, on my own the week after, with only Thomas in the house. I understood how to birth a bairn by then. By God, I'd had enough, and we needed no witnesses.

Thomas fetched Irene the next day. They swept in under cover of darkness and placed baby Donald in the cot with mine. He bore an uncanny resemblance to Francis, so I realised immediately who the father was. Irene was almost indistinguishable from me, my spitting image. Clearly, William couldn't resist. I couldn't tell Thomas and risk revealing my own secrets, and somehow it made sense I now had at least two bairns with dark curly hair. William's new wee bairn joined mine. Donald and Nellie—the twins who would never look alike.

During the war, William left to work out west. He resented the youngest boy, James, for killing his mother, and he left his second bairn, Catherine, only a child herself, to look after the rest of his brood.

Irene married Walter, the local groundsman at one of the big houses in Inveresk. They lived in, as she started the housekeeper job with him there, although she was expecting already. She fell fast, like her mother. I was happy she got settled and that William was out of our lives. I felt no need to let Donald know that his sister was really his mother. It would do no good for anyone.

SIXTEEN

RHIANNON

 Jan spotted me at the supermarket yesterday and shouted, 'Hiya!' as I made to leave. I was trying to avoid mad Tracey, who was serving her.

I mouthed, 'Hey', and gave a half-hearted wave back.

Jan's wave, an arm's length above her head, could not be missed. My hand had barely lifted above waist level. I couldn't pretend I'd never spotted her. She's not the type of person you miss. The whole store turned around when she yelled, and she beamed at them.

Loud and large, Jan fills a room with her personality as much as with her physical size. I gestured that I had to leave in a hurry. I hoped it seemed as if I had an appointment as I tapped my invisible watch. But I didn't have an appointment.

By the time I got home, Jan had added me on Facebook and asked if we could meet up. I've nothing to lose, I guess.

I've always appreciated Jan. She didn't originate

from the village. She grew up in the town and knew Kim from grammar school. She had worked with me in the village pub, along with Preston and Kim, in my first year of university holidays.

She was friendly, even though I was quite shy when I worked in the pub. The word 'shy' says a lot. As an adjective, it means to be retiring and wary of others, frightened and timid as in my youth. As a verb, it means to pull back, to dodge away from fear. That's what I do now. I'm the verb instead of the noun. My long-term loneliness has forced me to be shy again. I shy away.

SEVENTEEN
RHIANNON

I STROLL TO THE BENCH, getting my walk in before I meet with Jan. Kim is not there this time. As her name pops into my head again, I feel my mouth contort into a sneer.

I question why I had to meet her on my first day back. A sign? A warning? Foreboding worse things to come? Proof I can't hide from my past? She'd flown in like that single magpie, that crow.

I'd checked the population when I got home. Twenty thousand people live here now. This town is large enough for me to never bump into her again. But I'd felt an urge to find out all about Kim, so I ended up focusing on her, ambling around where I believed she might be.

Where does she live? I can't find her, although I expect her around every corner. When I saunter around town, every house I see, I wonder, *'Is this the one?* As if I expect her photo or a blue plaque on the wall outside.

Is this where she lives? She could be right behind those walls now.

I return to sit on the bench where I'd seen her before. Then I spy her across the street. I feel sick.

What if she sees me? She'll realise what I have been doing.

After turning off the alarm, she locks up the front door, as was always her habit.

From across the road, I notice she holds her arms straight down at the sides, with her bag in her left hand. It isn't a clutch. It has a dainty handle and a long handle hanging. She doesn't use the long strap to wear it as a cross-body bag or over her shoulder, as I might. She grips the short handle, as one might a bucket. It's identical to how she had carried her lunch box from the bench. Odd but familiar.

I glance at my phone, as if I'm busy, and note the time. Of course, it's five o'clock—the end of the working day. Kim was always punctual arriving and leaving work.

I watch her head through the alley at the side of the building.

Where did live? I can't even remember.

Where is she going now? To the car park? Or can she walk home now?

I am too nervous to follow her. I leave it a few minutes and then follow on through the vennel towards the car park and the council houses behind. The car park exits to a cobbled street beyond.

I've left it too long. I can't see her. Maybe she's already driven away. I head to the cobbled street, wondering if she's gone left or right. I'll be braver next time.

I glance behind me, as if Kim might lurk, ready to pounce out at me like she used to.

Then I abandon the plan, because I have to meet up with Jan at Debbie's café.

Debbie's café isn't a pleasant place. It's strictly a sit-down, eat, and go venue. Jan is late, so I stare out the window, considering others living their lives and sensing people peering back at me. I mess with my phone on social media for a while, and then I take out Great-great-granny Marie's journal and read it. I make myself socially unsociable so no one will talk to me—my mode of survival in public.

EIGHTEEN

Notes

MARIE, 1918

THOMAS CHANGED IN 1918. He left me alone altogether. I'd have no more children, thank God. The confident, arrogant minister had his heart ripped out. First by Irene and then Samuel.

The war did not end as fast as I had predicted. Soon, our sons were grown enough to fight ... and die. We put Samuel to rest, along with Minnie and William's boy, Johnny. The pals had travelled off to war together, and returned together, in boxes. They shared their funeral day in the same church in which their parents had wed.

The day before the boys' funerals, Thomas sat at his desk by the window while I sat in the chaise trying to sew, but, in reality, just staring. The sun shone on Thomas's face, making the age lines show more clearly than I had noticed before. Or perhaps it was because he was writing the eulogy for his own son's funeral.

'Did I tell you? I mean, did you know...?' His voice broke the silence like glass shattering. It was another of his 'Didn't you know?' stories from history. He uttered the phrase out of habit, not because he had something to say, as he always then searched for the next part of the sentence. He knew fine that I never knew anything. For all my lessons, I had never become a scholar.

He began, 'Lady Cockburn who lived in Ormiston Hall ...'

I glanced up

'Alison Cockburn?'

'Yes, you remember I told you about her a while ago?'

'I remember we visited the yew tree in the grounds of where she lived. You told me she was a great wit of her time.'

He managed a smile, clearly glad I remembered.

'She wrote a verse, a second part of The Flowers of the Forest,' he added.

'The Flooers o' the Forest,' I interrupted.

He smiled. I had corrected him with the Scots way of speaking, but his gentrified, university learning way was to anglicize everything.

'Yes, The Flooers.' It sounded alien. 'I found it in here.' He held up a book. I nodded as a request for him to read it and shut my eyes.

'I've seen the smiling
Of fortune beguiling,
I've tasted her pleasures
And felt her decay;
Sweet is her blessing,
And kind her caressing,
But now they are fled
And fled far away.'

I paused before I spoke again. 'Alison Cockburn didn't write the original words, though. Flodden was in 1513. She was not around for that. I mind she was friends with Rabbie Burns and David Hume,' I ventured.

Thomas nodded and gazed at me as he had way back when we visited the Mary's Mount stone.

'Well remembered, Marie.' He spoke my name aloud for the first time in years. 'Yes, she was around the time of Burns, and an admirer of Scott. He lived in the town for a while. Did you know he lived...?' His words tailed off.

'Yes, I know where he lived.'

He took a deep breath. I copied him, finding it incredible I could still breathe at all.

'So, Lady Cockburn's words, they were new words, a modern addition.'

No one but Thomas would deem something a hundred years old modern.

'What are the old ones, Thomas?'

'The former words from the Battle of Flodden?'

'Yes, tell me the words Mary Regina knew.'

He inhaled again, and then let another long sigh out. He didn't need to seek the words in the numerous books that lined the walls. Closing his eyes, Thomas recited them from memory.

'I've heard the lilting, at the yowe-milking,
Lassies a-lilting before dawn o' day;
But now they are moaning on ilka green loaning;
"The Flowers of the Forest are a' wede away".

Dool and wae for the order sent oor lads tae the
    Border!
The English for ance, by guile wan the day,
The Flooers o' the Forest, that fought aye the foremost,
The pride o' oor land lie cauld in the clay.'

'Read them tomorrow, Thomas. Read those ones,' I whispered.

He nodded and sat beside me, holding my hand as he had all those years ago. Then he leant his head on my shoulder and sobbed like a child.

NINETEEN

RHIANNON

JAN GRABS me and hugs me tight in front of everyone in apology when she arrives. Patrons in Debbie's are still nervous about that behaviour, granting us hard glares. Jan doesn't consider whether she's in my 'bubble' or whether hugs are allowed.

'Oh, you're looking well,' she exclaims, as she pulls up a seat at the table and I slip the closed journal back into my bag.

'And healthy,' she adds, as the former is often code for fatter, but I'm the opposite.

'You are looking well, too.' I return the compliment. She does appear well, and fatter—a huge lady who fills her whole size well.

'Oh, I'm feeling well. I'm the biggest I've ever been!' She seems delighted by this fact as she grabs a menu. 'What we having? Oh, so many treats and nice things. I'll have anything with cheese. Just bring a slab of cheese and a red wine, and I'm happy. I'm a cheap date, easy pleased. I swear that's all I need in life—that and staff. If I never had to dust in my life, that would suit me fine. I could do without that.' She takes a breath. 'And unloading the dishwasher. Every day, I stop and wonder how come I'm doing this again?' She laughs to the ladies next to us, encouraging them to join in.

Jan talks on until the food comes. She licks her lips and, before she takes a mouthful, announces, 'I tell you, if it wasn't for cheese, I'd be a size zero! I'd be built like the side of a fiver.' She barely breathes between pronouncements and mouthfuls. 'How've you been?'

I relate a brief summary of Colin, my work, and the flat.

'Oh yeah, you're in Preston's flat. Yeah, he got four years—aiding and abetting or perverting the course of justice or something. Dunno what the rule is in Scottish law. I only watch American cop shows. You basically cannae hide a dead body and get away with it. Every flat in the building overlooks the car park. The bin men would have found him in there at one point. It was his brother... apparently, the living room was a *mess*. Oh, sorry, are you no creeped out?'

'Nah.'

'Really? It would give me the heebie-jeebies. He'll be out in two years. They only serve half the sentence if they behave.'

'Well, he's done a year already.'

'God, is it that long since that all happened? Well, I guess we lost a year with the lockdown. Perfect time to be in prison when I think about it. We've all been in prison.' She changes the subject, quick as a bored man with a telly remote. 'I could kill someone ... I can understand Angela,' Jan announces.

'Who would you kill?' She thinks for a few seconds.

'Terry!'

'Really? You've been together for years.'

'I know, but why be in a relationship with someone you wouldn't want to kill now and then? How boring would that be?'

'How would you kill him?'

'He nearly went off the balcony in Magaluf one time, believe me. I'd kill him on holiday.' She snorts.

'So ... what would you do after you killed him?'

'Fly home.'

'I mean, how would you get off with it?'

'I'd deny it. Tell them I need to go as I've a plane to catch.'

'Of course.'

'And in their face, I'd say, "Who? I didn't even know him."' She smiles.

'You've lived with him for twenty years, Jan.'

She shrugs. 'Me? No! Don't know the man!'

I giggle. A smile feels like a strange action for the muscles on my face. I'm surprised they remember how to pull that expression. 'You can't say that.'

'Yeah, I can. I'd go totally blank. No idea who you mean? I've never seen that man—must have mixed me up with someone else.'

'The shared hotel room? The joint bank account?'

'Not me. It wasn't me. Memory loss.'

They would let her off for her cheek.

I NEVER WANTED to kill Colin. I never cared enough, even when I found out about the affair. I felt relieved, or it made sense, all the ignoring. Boredom had mentally moved me out of the relationship by then.

Jan jolts me back into the present. 'My plate is full,' she says.

I glance down for a second, thinking she refers to the empty plate in front of her, but then I realise she means a metaphorical plate.

'You know I've got Mum with me, right?' She changes the channel again. 'We're at that age. See, when you thought being an adult would be all fun and games and getting to do whatever you wanted. It never happened. Well, it did for about five years in my twenties, and then Terry happened, then kids, and now parents. Just as soon as the kids were off my hands, the parents got old. You need to take care of the oldies, and then you have to look after the twenty-year-olds that keep coming back, and in the middle, there's you. And no one is looking after you.'

I cringe. I have no children, and Mum isn't on my hands like Jan's mum is, but I've a need to visit, which is a type of bind, of course. I have to sort out a power of attorney for Mum and sell her house. I've already started moving out some of the belongings Mum packed up, but I do not have Jan's burden of caring for her full time. I agree with Jan, however, nodding.

We laugh a lot. Fast, fun and full of life, I can't understand why Jan wants to spend time with me. Eventually, I dare to mention Kim.

'Oh, not seen her for a while. It's been a couple of weeks. Oh, we used to have a laugh back in the pub, eh? Those were the days. Before kids and parents and emptying the dishwasher—ha, ha, ha. I wish the gang was all back there. It was the best time, wasn't it? That was when I felt free!'

I don't remember the pub in that way at all.

TWENTY

RHIANNON

BACK IN THE 1990S, people travelled for miles to be insulted at the pub where Kim, Jan, Preston and I worked. Preston performed as the star turn, but, for some reason, the bar owner and his son, Darren, didn't appreciate that Preston's antics were the main thing the bar had going for it. They hadn't renovated the place in years and took the local custom for granted. Being at the sharp end of Preston's jibes distracted from that.

Darren worked as the manager, though he carried out precious little work later on in the night, when he joined the guests in what he described as a 'host 'role. It meant he stopped working and got drunk. We got on well, but, for some reason, he was unsure of Preston. Preston was always popular with the girls, but Darren needn't have been jealous. Darren was handsome and enjoyed the popularity being a publican's son brought.

'Preston!' Darren shouted from the bar at opening time, scanning the restaurant and bar area. 'Preston!'

'Hiya! That is my name ... who wants to know?' Preston's head popped up from the floor, where he had been polishing the bar footrest.

'Can you change the barrels on that lager there?' Darren nodded towards the pumps. 'I'm struggling to get things done in here today.' He had a phone tucked under his chin with the cable stretched out and a clipboard in his hand.' I need to call the wholesalers. They haven't delivered the right order... again!'

'Aye, nae bother. Macho man to the rescue,' Preston announced to the few people who sat there so early in the morning. The elderly men rolled their eyes, and one lady giggled.

'Where is the wicked witch of the east, I wonder, when we need her?' Preston whispered as he pushed past me. I blushed and peeped around to see if Kim stood there. I had been under the impression Preston and Kim were friends.

'Don't know who you mean.' I picked up a cloth.

'Aye, you do!' He raised his eyebrows and nodded towards Kim coming through the door.

'Hmm.' He pursed his lips as he glanced back at me. 'And, right on cue, my pretty,' he muttered under his breath. He then opened the hatch down to the cellar, placed the fence around it to protect and warn everyone, and disappeared down there.

'Yeah, the delivery is wrong. I think we have someone else's,' Darren continued. He covered up the receiver. 'You are late,' he directed at Kim as she swanned past. Her face fell, and she shrugged and threw her bag down in the corner. She immediately painted on a smile and served a customer with a huge grin. Darren shook his head and smiled at me. I felt I had allies in the bar, who realised that Kim needed to be contained.

Preston returned and attended to a bald man and his large wife, who had sat down for a meal. They bickered as he approached. He hovered, hand on his hip and notebook poised, as they squabbled.

'Right! Enough of that. I've not got all day!' Preston barked, picking up the menus and placing them in their hands.

'Picking time!' he announced. His notorious rudeness seemed acceptable and taken as funny. I would never have been as brave. If I behaved in that way, I'd have been reported for ignorance. Preston could get away with murder.

'Everyone knows you'll pick the same as last week. Stop creating a palaver about it...! Come on! Chop, chop!'

The wife giggled.

'What's the special?' asked the man, piping up with a smile.

'Macaroni cheese with garlic bread.'

'I can make that in the house,' the wife declared.

'Can you now? Away you go, then. Cheerio.' Preston made to grab the menus out of their hands, but then handed them back with a grin, and they all laughed together.

'Okay, I'll have the steak.'

'One steak. And is that salad, veg, tatties or chips?'

'Salad'

'Salad? Are you sure, big boy? You've a figure to maintain,' Preston squealed as he patted the man's belly. Man and wife both roared.

'Come on! Go all out!' Preston ordered.

'Aye, all right. I'll have the chips.'

'Quite right, as predicted. And Madame ...?'

'I think I'll have lasagne and chips.'

'I don't think you *should* have the lasagne and chips,' her husband whispered across the table.

'Why not?'

'What happened to the diet?'

She pulled a face and shrugged.

'I remember when she had a figure. I remember when she actually had a waist.' He gestured to her, inviting Preston to comment, believing he might join in joking about his wife.

Preston paused and nodded, taking the menu off him. As he turned to walk away, he declared, 'Do you, aye? Mmm. And she remembers when you had hair.'

They both howled. Even the man nodded in agreement, patting his head. This was what they had come for!

More tables joined in as the audience. One young man of around twenty was the loudest.

Preston stopped dead and faced him. 'And I dinnae ken what you're laughing it. You can come back here and laugh at folk when you sport a haircut that doesn't match the 'one you mother gave you when you started school.'

I smiled at Darren, who was scowling. 'Come on, he is funny.'

'Why do all the girls like him?'

'He's safe, and you've nothing to worry about. The girls like you too.'

'Really?'

'Really.'

He reached out and touched my hand. 'Do you?'

I sighed and felt myself redden.

'Yeah.' I spotted Kim over his shoulder and withdrew my hand.

He turned, noticing her too, and ambled through the back.

'Getting pally with the boss's son, eh?' she asked.

'No. Not particularly'

'Particularly? Dinnae see the point of you being here *particularly*. Not like you'll want to stay on. This place will not be *particularly* good enough for you, will it? Not posh enough for the student? I think students are a burden *particularly*. Lying about all day doing nothing while normal folk are working, thinking they're better than everyone else. I don't see the point of it all. *Particularly ...*'

'It's because I have exams, and Mum said ...'

'Mm-hmm. Don't see the need. I mean, *particularly*'—she smirked—'if you are hanging about around here. You should go up the town and be done with it, away from us peasants.'

Darren returned, and Kim grinned at him and straightened herself up, sticking out her ample chest with her blouse cut down as far as possible. She owned the classic barmaid appearance, all tits, teeth, and red lips.

'All right, Kim?' He spoke to her cleavage.

'Yes, I'm very all right, Darren,' she flirted.

He hesitated and then turned to me. 'Rhiannon, would you come and help me with this order? It's still no right.'

Kim's face screwed up like a crumpled ball of paper as she watched us sneak through the back corridor. Darren squeezed my hand. The van wasn't there, and when it did arrive, ten minutes later, Kim must have noticed it, realising he had used it as a ruse to get me alone.

LATER, Darren, after he had been drinking, observed me giggling with Preston and shouted over. 'Preston!'

'Whaaaaaaaat? What you wanting?' Preston yelled back

'Here, I never knew you had a brother.'

Preston stopped. and his mouth screwed up as if he had tasted something sour. 'And?'

'Well, someone at the bar mentioned you had a brother, that's all.'

Kim had a smug expression on her face. 'His name is Red.' She butted in. Preston fired her a sharp glance. She rolled her eyes and continued stacking glasses.

'I never told you about my sister either.'

'Right ... what's your sister's name, something red as well?' Darren smirked, scanning for support.

Kim smiled at him.

Preston carried on cleaning glasses. 'Aye, that's right. Strawberry.'

'What? But your surname, what is it?'

'Field ...'

'Strawberry Field? Are you joking?' He snorted, but Preston cut him off.

'Of course, I'm joking. For fuck's sake. That's stupid.'

'Oh, right. What is it then?'

'Tatiana.'

'Tatiana? From around here?' He threw him a mocking look.

'Aye.'

'Tatiana Field? Pfft.' Kim glanced up again and opened her

mouth to speak. Preston indicated her to be quiet by putting his finger up at his mouth. Darren glanced at her, and Preston strode out into the bar area.

'Aye, the family call her Tati for short.' As he continued on, dawdling about, he announced, 'I'm away to wipe the tables.'

Preston waited.

'Oh, for God's sake, Preston,' Darren exclaimed. Kim and I cracked up as the penny dropped with Darren. 'Tati field! You don't half talk some shite. ... Tati Bloody Field! Yer nothing but a bloody liar.' Darren stormed out.

'My work here today is done! Glad I came in now.' Preston folded his cloth and threw it, with style, onto his shoulder.

LATER, Darren wandered back in, avoiding Preston's eye.

'Just need to sort out some stuff out back. It will take two of us again'. He winked at me, and we enjoyed another few minutes together, leaving Kim and Preston manning the bar. I returned along the corridor to hear Jan, who had arrived after her dental appointment.

'Thank God you're here!' shouted Preston

'Here comes the cavalry. Where is everyone?' I heard her ask, as I skulked back towards the bar.

'Our Romeo and Juliet are out the back, sorting out the order.' His fingers put inverted commas round the sorting out the "order" parts. He stared right at me, with his back to the bar.

'Oh, here she is now ... oooh!' Preston exclaimed as he jumped. Kim slammed down a man's pint so hard with a bang that she ended up spilling it.

'Kim, oooh!' he responded again. Then he leant forward to, Jan, who cackled as always at any drama, and stage whispered, 'Someone's nose is out of joint!'

TWENTY-ONE
RHIANNON

I HAVE TO VISIT MUM. *Have* to—not *want* to.

I'm not a devoted daughter like Jan, but I have a box of Mum's personal belongings from the house that want going through with her, so I work myself up to visit that decrepit, Victorian place at the edge of town.

Preston used to work there, in the kitchen of this old folk's home, and Jan told me Angela volunteered there too.

When I arrive, Lesley, a pretty girl on reception, says from behind a screen, 'Hiya. How are you?' She doesn't wait for a reply.

'You need to sign in. We've got COVID rules in here still. And sanitise.' She sings her instructions and appears delighted about it all.

People are starting to march right past hand gel dispensers now, but here, the rules are still strict and most comply. I wander along the corridor to Mum's room at the rear in the annex.

Mum isn't capable now. Sometimes she's lucid and at other times confused. She comes up with stories about real events but confuses them with shows on television or things she wished had happened. She tells tales of how this famous actor asked her out, even though he couldn't have. It's a different actor the next time she tells it.

As I enter, she glances up then focuses back on the television, where an Elvis Presley movie is playing. She tells me all about it, without even a greeting.

'This lassie here—that one, the girl—is making out she does not love him.' She nods at me with a smirk. 'See him. He's singing. Handsome, eh? And see her face? Ooh, see her looking at him now.' She giggles. 'You watch. I reckon she fancies him, and you'll see. Uh-huh, they'll get together. Oh yes, you mark my words.'

I've seen it, or one similar to it, many times before, and so has she. That's exactly what happens. The *Mills and Boon* books by her bedside tell a similar story, nearly all of them.

'I don't like this room, Rhiannon.' She sniffs, while Elvis sings.

'Why? It is the same as all of them. I pick up a pillow from a chair and lay it to the side, so I can sit. 'And it's quiet at the back of the building.'

'Do you remember Agnes Moleman?'

I shrug.

'You must? She lived in the village, across the road. Moved to the town later.'

'Yes,' I say because I've heard the name numerous times, and I remember her being pointed out to me.

Mum realises I'm being vague. Sometimes, she notices my thoughts written all over my face, despite her issues.

'Yes, you do. She was the teacher at the school in the town. Never married. She was engaged to a fella once, but he died. Anyway, this was Agnes' room, and Angela, that lassie what killed that man, was in here the day before she died. She was in visiting her, right here. Lesley said.'

'Who's Lesley?' I ask, immediately regretting it.

'The lassie at the desk, with the squeaky voice. Lesley maintained Angela never had anything to do with it, although I doubt it. Agnes died that very night.'

'Ah, gee whizz, Mother! What age was she, though? A hundred?' I snort.

'No. Agnes wasn't that old.'

'Wasn't she?' I stand and stare out the window. I breathe in to carry on talking, but I don't continue. I know the next progression for Mum is her leaving here like Agnes.

Her favourite topic to talk about is the village. People I have long forgotten, ones I never met, and family relations, Mum will explain in minute detail, as if I should remember everything about them. I've heard all her stories a million times, and they are told the same way, with no deviation. They are comforting pathways of words that trip off her tongue, rhythmically, like poetry. It's not the words she utters that help her; it's the soothing, familiar cadence, the pattern—she knows what word comes next. She experiences no confusion then. Her tongue recites them, like muscle memory, without her even having to consider them. When I dare mention Kim, her face screws up.

'Her! I never liked that bairn. She wasn't right. Do you mind her?'

How can she forget that I know Kim well?

'Forward she was. Awfully confident, bloody cocky even. No wonder, with a mother like that. You know her mother, Maureen, married Alec. He was a lot older than her. Aye, he was your nana Annie's age. He'd never married, but he won some money, and she was right in there. Alec hated me. I won the gala day race, and I marched up to claim my prize, and he gave it to Rena instead. I won that race, but he pretended he never noticed me. My mother said to ignore him and come away.

'"Brush the dust from your feet," she used to say. They never cared for us that lot.'

Content that my mother hates Kim, too, I let her rant on.

'Maureen was a right cow.'

I know it to be my mother's word for a promiscuous woman.

'How she fancied herself—I don't know why. Her fireplace was a mess.'

At the comment, I glance up and smile.

'Always pranced about like lady muck,' Mum continues, 'looking as if she came brand-new out of a box, but the ashes in the fire could come out to meet you at the door. She hadn't cleaned them out in so long.'

It was such a strange turn of phrase. Now, no one cared about the state of a person's fireplace, or even understood it as an insult, it was so old-fashioned. But back in the village, owning the cleanest fireplace and front step mattered.

'That Kim. She'd come round begging to babysit. I'd never let her. Maureen let them run free, Kim and her wee brothers and sister. She wouldn't take no for an answer. She kept coming.' Mum mimicked her voice. 'Can I take Rhiannon out? Can I watch Rhiannon?'

I drift off, staring out of the window, letting her go on, thinking about how to broach the subject of selling the house. There isn't much to see, just a wall with the trees beyond in view. I can hear football in the playing fields across the way. It takes me back to the park with Kim, one of my earliest memories.

Mum rambles on about the neighbours and who slept with whom, none of it news to me. Who slapped whom on their wedding day for cheating on their man. Who caught whom with another man's wife.

I always remember the hurt and the bad memories from the village. I don't recall the fun and laughter. Pain seems easier to cling to; those nerve receptors ping harder and stronger than any pleasure centres. I feel content when I remember the happy times, but no elation, no jubilation. Joy pierces my skin only superficially. Horror is injected much deeper.

'I eventually let her take you out,' Mum prattles on. 'Do you remember? You'll not remember. I gave up and let her, as you were getting under my feet.'

I REMEMBER. Kim took me to the park. She never spoke all the way there, instead towing me along and then letting me run with the other children. I was five, and she was ten.

I played on the swings as Kim and her friends, some older girls and boys, sat on the bench

'I need the toilet, Kim,' I whined, running up to her.

She gave an acid smile. 'Shut up, stupid.'

Her friends giggled.

I ambled back to the playground. Then I returned to bleat again, 'But Kim, I really need ...'

'I said SHUT UP!'

And then I couldn't hold on any longer, and my dress got wet and hot, and then cold. I ran with the noise of their screaming and howling in my ears, all the way home. I ran as fast as possible, and she barked a laugh that emanated from deep in her gut. It contained no empathy and was not at all forced.

She arrived back at our house a few minutes after I did, and announced, 'She just ran away. She never said she needed to go, Mrs—'

'Rhiannon, you should have said,' Mum tsked. I watched Kim smirk, peering past my mother at me.

I also remembered the fire in which Kim's mother and siblings all perished. Although that must have taken place on a different day, somehow the memories merged. I'm not sure whether I remember because I saw it, or because Mum told me about it. But I stood with Kim when it happened. I can see it, can feel the heat. Not only the fire, but both of us, me holding Kim's right hand after a visit to the park, as her family burned to death.

'KIM WAS A RIGHT A SLAPPER, cheating on her man,' Mum goes on, and I am jolted back to now with the mention of her name.

'You mean Maureen,' I reply, sitting again.

'No, I mean Kim. The mother was Maureen.'

I shake my head. Kim was a tart, too, but Mum mixes them up.

'Then he died ... makes you think.'

'No Mum. Maureen died, Mum, in the fire.' She must be tired.

'Callous. Hard as nails. Made of steel. And a tramp with all the men, her. Even when she was married to that boy who died.'

'Old Alec?'

'What? Not, Alec! The boy. I can't remember his name.'

I wonder if she knows what she says. She seems certain.

'The boy who died in the pub.'

'What do you mean, the pub? Kim worked in the pub with Darren and me. Maureen and her three kids died in the fire. Only Alec and Kim were left.' I groan.

'Oh yes, the fire. Never forget that day. I didn't know where you were, but it turned out Kim was with you.' Mum shuts her eyes.

I take out the wooden box I found in a box of books in the house. It's locked, so I figure it is something important. *What's the chance Mum will remember where the key is?* I think. I probably should just throw it in the fire, except that it might contain the deeds or something.

'Mum, I'm clearing out the house,' I begin.

Her eyes snap open again. 'Your house?'

'No, yours.' I hold up the box, something inside it shifts and thunks. 'I found this. Do you want to keep it? Do you know what's inside?'

Mum stares at it for a minute. 'Something of Nettie's,' she says. 'Or maybe Granny's.'

'Do you have a key?'

She shakes her head, and her lips tremble. Then she lifts a wrinkled hand and points to her dresser drawer. 'Not unless it's in there.'

Nothing of importance gets left in the care home. Everything there vanishes over time, so I'm sceptical, but I tug open the drawer and navigate reading glasses and an old case for dentures and nightgowns. There is nothing else.

'No,' I say. 'Should I bin it?' I rattle the box again.

'It's a flimsy lock,' Mum says. 'Surely you can break into that.'

TWENTY-TWO
RHIANNON

IN 1992, when the pub fancy dress night came around. I felt ill, but I turned up to work anyway, not wanting to leave them short staffed. The outfits we wore made the events seem surreal and ridiculous.

Staff had been given the theme of *Alice in Wonderland*. The fancy dress was Kim's idea, so she chose the Queen of Hearts, the most flattering costume. As the youngest, I was allocated Alice by Darren, which Kim objected to.

'Can she not be that slug thing?' Kim suggested with disgust.

'Slug? What slug? You mean the caterpillar?' Jan asked.

'I dunno. Some insect. I never read the thing. I only saw the film.'

Preston and Jan dressed as Tweedledum and Tweedledee.

'Trust me to be the fat one,' yelled Jan, as she hauled on the costume. Darren took the Mad Hatter costume.

Jan and Kim took a break, leaving Preston and I to man the bar ourselves. We'd finished food service by then, so it could have been worse. Preston's antics took my mind of my grumbling tummy for a while.

'Where are those other two?' He scanned the bar area.

'Out the back, having a fag.'

He tutted and made to go find them, when one of the customers interrupted.

'Preston?' The punter leaned on the bar. He was a straight guy but fascinated by Preston. 'How come you're single?'

'Och, dinnae ask.'

'Come on. What happened to the last guy?'

'He hated me, that was about it. It was all fine and dandy at the beginning, but then he stopped coming round. I ended up way down the priority list, after all his baggage.'

'What baggage?'

'Let's just say he had more baggage than Jenner's luggage department.'

'What like?'

'Ex-wives.'

'Wives?'

'Four of them!'

'But ... wives?'

'Aye, you heard me. And old boyfriends and children. God knows how many children he had. I lost count. He wanted his cake, eat it, and a slice of everybody else's cake a'naw.'

There was sniggering at the bar. Preston turned to another customer. 'Your usual? Double G and T?' Then he turned back to the original 'audience' member. 'Then there was the cat fiasco.'

'The cat?'

'What's this about a cat?'

'His boyfriend's cat.'

More gave their attention to Preston's story.

'Aye, the excuses not to come around got worse and worse. If it wisnae he was washing his hair or cutting his nails, he was bloody filing his taxes. The last straw was the cat. He looked after this cat for his neighbour, who was in the hospital. The cat was wild, he said, creating havoc in his house. He maintained he couldn't come over for three months as he couldn't leave it. Something about it getting trapped behind the fridge and shite.'

'Okay...'

'Then, one day, I lost it. I complained and asked why he couldn't stay over. Do you know what he said? I can't stay over. The cat might set the house on fire.'

'Eh?' questioned one listener.

'Said it deadpan, in all seriousness.'

'How? How does a cat set a house on fire?'

'That's what I said.'

'But how?'

'Search me! And he repeated it, as if that happened all the time. I thought, am I in some parallel universe here, where this is a thing?'

'But how could a *cat* set a house on *fire*?'

'I dunno. Maybe chew the electrics at the back of the fridge that it was always getting trapped under, I suppose.'

I pictured a cat nipping up to the co-op and buying a set of firelighters and packet of Swan Vesta matches. I couldn't pull a pint for giggling. Preston noticed, and with a sparkle in his eyes and a twitch of his lips, he carried on.

'A wee pyromaniac cat flicking a lighter at the window as the guy leaves saying, "Meow make my day."'

I handed over the pint, shaking my head, but my customer's attention was on Preston, so I stood with my hand out as she ignored me. She howled, fuel for Preston's fire, and he turned up the heat. He sang, 'Just a wee cat, the wee, mad, arsonist pussy threatening to burn the whole joint down as soon as anyone's back was turned. A wee, crazy psychopath cat with a blackmailing controlling personality.'

The laughter rose.

'What kinda fucking cat was it?'

'Just a wee grey cat. It was a step too far. I told him I'd heard some bullshit in my life, but that took the biscuit. Not only the biscuit, the whole packet of Hobnobs. I just said, "That's it. I'm off." So that was that.' Preston started giggling, bent over the bar, his shoulders shaking.

'What is it?' I asked.

'I just remembered the cat's name...!' He gasped.

'Aye, what was it?'

'Smokey!'

The bar audience groaned while we carried on working without Kim and Jan.

'You look like shite.' Preston motioned to me, as I caught myself in the mirror. Sweating hot and cold, I agreed with his assessment.

'I feel ... Oh, I have to go.' I bolted to the toilet, my stomach grumbling and growling.

'Oh, that's fine! You all leave me on my own,' Preston called after me.

I passed Darren, who glanced up from his position chatting in the corner with some regulars.

I ran to the toilet and sat down heavily, feeling dizzy and sick. After being violently ill, I sat for a while staring at the black-and-white tiles. After a few minutes, I made a move to clean myself up at the sink. I returned to the cubicle, shoved the seat down, and pulled my feet up on top of the lid, curling in a ball. I leant my face again the cubicle, feeling the cold, hard wall against my face and shut my eyes.

The muffled rumble of music from the bar in the distance, with its indistinct bass-line thumping, became loud and clear as the door opened, and Kim and Jan barged in.

They should not have been drinking on shift, but Kim and Jan had already had a few. I didn't feel like coming out, in case they shouted at me for leaving Preston on his own, even though they were as guilty with their ever-extending break. They flew in and used the cubicles, shrieking at each other across my middle trap. As they both exited their respective cubicles, they chatted.

'Here, what you think about Rhiannon and Darren?' Jan giggled.

'Alice and the Mad Hatter!'

'Ooh, kinky.'

'Social climber, her. She thinks she's perfect, but I'm the Queen!' proclaimed Kim.

'She is all right.'

'Nut! Trying to get her claws into Darren, the tramp.' I heard the snap of a powder case, and figured Kim was reapplying her lipstick.

'Oh Kim, you are terrible,' giggled Jan.

'Always thought he preferred me, but there you go. Seems he is slumming it with Plain Jane Rhiannon. I mean, how could he resist me?'

I peered through the crack in the door as they screamed and shook their boobs in the mirror. Kim pulled her top down to expose her cleavage. I kept quiet. I couldn't come out now.

'I'll snare him, and once he's had a real woman, he won't want that bore.' She cackled as she washed her hands.

'You could marry him,' suggested Jan, 'in that outfit.'

'I think I will. I'll be the landlady of the pub, queen of the village.'

'Then what?

'Well, then that bawheid would need to watch himself on the stairs.' I heard them screech, and the music from the bar became clear and then muffled as they opened and closed the door on their way out.

I CREPT OUT SOON after and washed my face again. Then, once back in position, I carried on serving while Kim collected glasses. I watched her dance with Darren, the life and soul of the party. I stared as she led him outside, and I watched through the glass while Preston bantered on.

'And you? Are you the knees on the bees?' Preston babbled on.

They didn't even hide their embrace.

I saw Kim lead Darren across the road to her house, and I heard the volume of the laughter and music in my ears become deafening as the queasy hot and cold feeling crawled all over me again.

TWENTY-THREE

RHIANNON

OUT WALKING AGAIN, I stroll to the cobbled street ahead of Kim at the correct time. If she is on foot, I hope she'll turn right as I stand to the left of the junction. I devise my getaway plan.

The church gate is open, and I can sneak in there if she turns left towards me. I wait—no, lurk.

There she is, wearing a black-and-white checked scarf. She turns right. I can follow, but I freeze, feeling glued to the ground. I watch Kim walk as far as the roundabout and then turn left. I unstick my feet and rush on just as she vanishes from sight. The road leads to the river, and it is then a left or right turn along the bank or straight over the bridge. When I reach the roundabout, I still can't see her, so she hasn't gone across the bridge, at least. Houses line the bank, so she could be heading into one of them.

I walk towards the river. If she spots me, I can stroll across the bridge. There's no reason I shouldn't be wandering along here. It's a well-known route. I view the left side—some houses and more on the right. I spot Kim in the distance marching along on the right. I try to stay around without obviously loitering.

As if waiting for a call, I glance at my phone, but then I follow when she seems far enough away. If she turns back, she might notice me. It's cold enough to justify pulling my hoodie up, so I do.

Why did I wear this? With Strathclyde University written on the front, it's a dead giveaway. Everyone knows I graduated from Strathclyde. I remind myself on Messenger to buy a plain hoodie. Along the river to the left is a grassy area. To the right are houses with streets coming off. Some streets pass through to the roads on the far side; others are cul-de-sacs, dead ends. Kim turns up one of those. I can't make out which one, but quite far along. At the end of this road is a park, and then the lagoons stretch out. A sea wall and path hug the water and wild land for birds is further inland. Dog walkers love it.

Kim must live in one of the streets off this road, I think, *perhaps the third*. Beyond that, I can't see, so I turn back and saunter home across the bridge. She lives minutes away from me, over the river.

Maps on the Internet show me six openings off this road by the river. No one goes along here unless they are going to a house in this area or to enjoy the lagoons. I guess it isn't the first three openings, as I could see that far. It is likely one of the last three, but with her so far in the distance, I didn't make out which. A search tells me they're called The Avenue, The Terrace, and The Gardens. The nearest two lead to the far away parallel road. I hope that is not where she was headed because then I'll have further twists and turns to negotiate.

I buy a plain hoodie online—a grey one to match the weather.

TWENTY-FOUR

RHIANNON

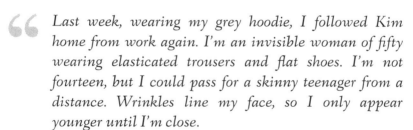 Last week, wearing my grey hoodie, I followed Kim home from work again. I'm an invisible woman of fifty wearing elasticated trousers and flat shoes. I'm not fourteen, but I could pass for a skinny teenager from a distance. Wrinkles line my face, so I only appear younger until I'm close.

I dared follow her further along the river and saw that she turned into the last opening before the park, into The Gardens. I watched her head towards one of the semi-detached houses on the left of the cul-de-sac.

In the street, she kissed a man on the cheek before she entered the house. Kim's man was out washing their car. He was certainly an upgrade on Darren from the village, who we'd fought over before.

This new chap, conservatively dressed in a V-neck sweater, looked shiny and clean. I bet he smelt nice. He had a smiley face, cheeks like pinchable apples with a dimpled chin and silver hair. Fat? Yes, but pleasantly so. He seemed familiar, but I couldn't place him.

Kim's house is expensive looking. How she can afford it? Her wage can't be huge. He must have a well-paid job. A lot of women want a man with money.

He chose her. She's made a fair choice, and he wanted her.

TWENTY-FIVE
RHIANNON

MUM IS right about the box. I manage to bust it open easily enough and we go through its contents together at the care home. They're disappointing—broken old costume jewellery and a wad of faded letters from Granny Irene, writing down memories for her daughters.

The 'clunking' was a small, leather-bound journal my grandmother Annie, Mum's mother, had kept.

'Have you read any of this before? Anything interesting?' I ask Mum, not convinced the letters or diary are worth my while.

Mum shakes her head. 'I don't remember.'

She unfolds one of the faded old letters with her faded old fingers. 'I suppose you better read them to me.'

I pick up the oldest looking one and start.

Dearest Nettie,

When you asked me to write down a little more about my life in service before I forgot it all, I did not realise how difficult it would be, firstly to remember it at all, but also to set it down in black and white. Still, I have done my very best, but I do feel perhaps it is best fit for fireplace after your eyes only.

Of course, by now you know about William and what happened between he and I. Well, after he left, I expected that he had gone from our lives forever—from mine and from mother's. Instead, he returned to the village in 1926 with a young wife and two young daughters. The tall, broad wife he brought from the west was course and rough as guts. Famie, the oldest daughter, bore her mother's unfortunate sharp features and hulking build.

I saw him across the street in passing. He was fatter and lined, but still a handsome man. I could barely stand it. He knew my secret; however, as time passed, I got power from it. Our child was his secret, too, and we eyed each other when we passed.

William had nothing to do with the family he abandoned. James had been getting on fine without his drunkard father. James worked in in the mill in the main town, a mere walk along the river from the village, and had married Helen. He didn't need his father back bothering him for money, which William did all the time, as he never worked. William maintained James should keep him, for bringing him up that short time.

I'd spend time with Helen when we had seasonal work in the market garden, and she'd work for extra money, bringing young Harriet with her. Harriet would play with the two boys from the big house in the summer, with my Annie and my three younger ones—all getting along before adulthood would separate their lives by class.

IN 1929, Famie came to work with us in service at the big house. She was barely fourteen, and I never sensed the extent of the trouble she would cause. I had to act Christian, and it took all of my power to even employ her, but we needed local girls for the house. I tried so hard not to treat her differently because of her father, but the girl was easy to dislike. She was a lumbering, stupid girl with little concentration who was able to work only with much encouragement or downright, continual nagging. One must be agile in service; she lumped around instead, sometimes waking the master. She understood she should crawl in and light the fire without wakening him, but a herd of elephants would have made less noise.

'Famie!' I exclaimed one day when she stood, immobilised, over a smashed plate.

'Euphemia!' I used her Sunday name, and she jumped to attention. 'What have you done now? Honestly, the sooner you are married off and kept the better, out from under my feet.'

She never moved. 'That'll be coming out your wages,' I continued.

'I fancy getting married,' she remarked, staring into nowhere.

'What?' I bent to pick up the pieces. She certainly wasn't moving to help in any way. I stood up and pointed. 'Pick that up,' I demanded. It was her job to clean up her mess, not mine.

'Oh, right,' she mumbled. She wasn't the type of girl who acted without being told. 'One day, I think I will. I'll get married.'

I threw her a disparaging glance.

'Will you?' I guffawed, wondering who'd suffer that daft, hulking brute of a girl. 'Who'd have you?' I voiced aloud.

'How about Donald?' she mused as she stood.

'*My* Donald?' I reddened, nearly giving him away as my son.

'Yes, your brother.'

I paused. The look she gave me made me wonder whether she knew the truth. Maybe more thoughts existed in that head than it seemed. He couldn't marry Famie. They were both William's bairns. Did she know? Was she testing me? I got a grip of myself, beckoning her to follow me with the broken pieces. She needed to be led. I'd have been better clearing it up myself, by the time it took me in telling her what to do.

'He's only fifteen.' I had to ensure they kept apart. Donald resembled William, but I could not conjure up any further similarities. Donald had the gentle manner of my father, and the kindness of an angel. He made everyone feel they could do better, be better. I sensed he'd never marry; Donald was not the marrying type.

Marie—or mother, as he and I knew her—would be the only woman Donald would love. He adored her, but he never gave women or girls in general a glance.

'One day, though.' Famie followed me, still wittering on, dropping bits of broken plate and picking them up again.

'No!' I bit.

'Why not?'

I turned on the stairs and grabbed her arm and shook it. 'Because you're a clumsy oaf and common as muck,' I shouted. She looked shocked by my outburst. She had never seen me lose control. I gathered myself, as I turned to continue downstairs, but I heard her mutter, 'Something funny about him anyway.'

I THOUGHT she'd forgotten about her silly idea. It wasn't until 1932, when Famie persuaded Donald to help her with her reading, that I realised she still had it in mind. He took pity on the girl, as a kindness, and she took it as an invitation to take advantage. She was a year younger than him, but years and lifetimes ahead in slyness. She wasn't just stupid, she was wicked, but he refused to see it.

I turned up at the manse, where Donald stood with mother in the hallway, and spied Famie seated in the front room.

'What is she doing here?' I muttered to mother

'She is harmless, uneducated. She wanted some help with reading,' whispered Donald.

'Her?'

Mother shrugged her shoulders.

'She's trying to better herself, I suppose.' She didn't sound convinced.

'At least we can do something to help her, no?' suggested Donald.

I spoke with mother awhile as Donald entered the front room to the daft lassie. As I left, I listened at the door. Cracked it open just a little and spied her and the back of Donald. Her voice was raised, her face red.

'I'll tell them what you are, like! You are not right! I'll make sure everyone knows. It's against God—that's what it is.' She stormed past me. I barged into the room and interrogated him.

'What is she saying? What happened?'

He shook his head and sat down

'She's got the wrong idea about me. About me … and her. Leave her.'

My mother always said my temper came from my red hair. I ran after Famie, catching up with her in the road. I pulled her back around to face me. She raised her nose in the air and crossed her arms. 'What's your business?' She snarled.

'What are you up to?'

'What do you mean?'

'With Donald,' I said.

'That Donald from the manse?' She laughed. 'Your Donald? Isn't it funny he looks nothing like his father? Funny that.'

She knew. She understood, and she didn't care until he rejected her.

'He's been leading me on.'

'He hasn't,' I spat. 'As if! He's got a girl in Edinburgh,' I came up with, thinking in a hurry.

She wasn't falling for that one. 'No, he's not. He told me he hasn't any girl. No girl at all. He's not like that. There'll be no girl there!' She worked up to a crescendo, her voice higher and higher pitched.

When I stopped, she appeared triumphant.

'Turns out he is a Nancy boy.'

'You can't say that.'

'Oh, I'll say it, and I'll tell everyone. And I'll tell that's not his father nor his mother.'

'You can't do that. You won't do that,' I softly reminded her. I had the upper hand again.

She tightened her lips, realising she couldn't tell that secret without outing her own father too. 'But I'll tell them all the minister's so-called son is an abomination. I'll tell everyone.'

'Be quiet!' I screamed.

'I will not,' she shouted, backing away. 'I'll say it, and believe me, the dogs will bark it by the time I finish ruining the lot of you!'

I stood still, although I wanted to chase after her and claw her eyes out. I was stuck to the spot, my hands on my hips and my thumbs burrowing into my back.

I should have chased her right there and then, and things may have turned out differently. Instead, I spun and spotted Donald leaning against the tree. He'd heard it all.

NEWS of the boy on the railway line came on a Tuesday, but I sensed who he was before they told me. He was gone—my son who I mourned as my brother. I realised why. He would be the talk of the Steamie due to Famie. He would have brought shame on the family. Though I don't believe he died of shame. He died from being too perfect for this world, from not understanding the hatred in others.

I entered the church on that rainy Tuesday to pray. I prayed for peace—abroad in the world and in our streets—for all the use that made. Peace could never come, not to the world, not to the foreign fields, and not even to our village. Too many things had happened in the past, never forgotten, old feuds and curses reappearing. The slate is never clean. The past keeps returning, not for us to learn from to gain peace, but to learn to hate all over again. We have seen too much history to stop turning the wheel.

Even as I walked out of the church with a prayer for peace on my lips, I vowed Famie would pay.

I'll write some more another time. That's enough for now to be going on with.

All my love,

Irene (Mum) xoxo

TWENTY-SIX
RHIANNON

I'VE PLANNED to meet Jan again. This time, it's a longer walk away —two miles along the river to the village. We meet in the pub we used to work in together. I haven't been in it since that Christmas 1992. I returned for the Christmas holidays, and by that time, Kim and Darren were engaged. Kim appeared triumphant.

I never wanted to return to the pub, realising Darren and Kim lived there together. I couldn't work there, so I decided I'd find some other work over the holidays.

'I try to eat healthy, but with Terry, it's impossible!' Jan babbles. 'His plate has not a vitamin in sight. He's Glaswegian, you see. I don't think he ever saw a banana until he went to university, as if it were wartime. He thinks ketchup is a vegetable. He is a sugar-addict. Hell, the unhealthy eating doesn't stop. Bread and crisps for lunch. Carbs for dinner. I tell him Rich Teas biscuits don't count after cutting out the sugar in the tea. Then a chocolate later on, sticky toffee pudding, and a cappuccino every meal. Then he moans he can't sleep after three coffees and enough sugar to set a toddler climbing the walls. He's an addict, I tell you. It's crack to him.' Jan barely breathes before she goes on. 'It's a fine line from wanting to live longer to thinking "Oh, to hell with it, life's too short."'

The latter is clearly winning, and Terry is a feeder.

'I want a salad and try to eat healthy, then he buys me gifts of sweets. He's got the diabetes now, so he needs to fix himself, but he won't listen.'

I try to get a word in, but I can't.

Jan changes the subject. 'I loved working here.' She gazes around. 'Where's Darren these days?'

She stares at me in silence. 'He died,' she whispers.

'No! What?'

How didn't I know? Is that what Mum meant about the boy in the pub dying? I imagined Mum was just getting muddled up. I couldn't remember her telling me before, but I hadn't been listening properly for years.

I blanch and find myself suddenly unable to swallow my drink. Arrogant, cocky Darren is dead. We'd shared a moment together. I'd loved him for a few weeks.

Jan sighs. 'God ... you didn't know? It was a while ago, hen.'

'Kim and he were still going strong when I left.'

'Well, she got the pub, of course, and then sold it. So she's rich—sorted for money. She kept her job, though she can't need the money.'

'What happened to Darren?'

'Fell down the cellar. Kim found him. The gate wasn't up, for some reason. Kim said she was always telling him, but he must have forgotten to put it up and left the hatch open.'

I listen, aghast, all the hairs on my arms standing up.

'I remember it was funny at the time, 'cos I was in the pub after it all happened, and the barrels weren't needing changed. I remember Preston saying that everything was all up to date too.'

She clearly doesn't remember Kim threatening to knock him down the stairs the night they got together. She hasn't made that connection, not in all that time. I stare over at the bar; it's the same but different. I don't know the people manning the bar now. They're younger folk from the village, not my generation.

'Fell?'

'Yeah, he fell down the cellar. Right there.' Jan gestures towards the scene of the crime. 'Kim found him when she came in from work. She'd started work at the accountants by then. She said being the pub landlady wasn't for her. Were you not here? I can't believe you didn't know this.'

'No. I'd moved away by then.' I can't take my mind of Darren's death.

Kim wouldn't have? She couldn't have? For the money? The pub?

It didn't seem enough.

WHEN JAN LEAVES to drive home, I insist on walking—no, hiking —the few miles home. It's a sunny day, in contrast to the dark news I have just received, so I stop in to the old folks' home. I often feel guilty about Mum now, after seeing Jan and listening to her woes.

Mum seems in fine spirits at first, but she starts nodding off as I read another letter from the box, upon request.

IRENE, 1937

Dearest Nettie,

Here is another installment, as promised. Keep it close to your chest!

Famie still worked with us in 1937. I couldn't unload her onto anyone. She'd never married; as predicted, no man would take her either.

I settled into barely disguised, hated tolerance. William and his family had moved from the miners' cottages to the newly built houses called 'The Road', so it became apparent they never planned on moving away. They fell on their feet with modern, clean houses with inside toilets. My daughter Annie joined service with me as soon as she turned fifteen.

Working at the house was warm and clean, compared to the mine carts. There was not much pay for a fifteen-year-old, but free food and a half-day holiday every fortnight, all for polishing silver, dusting, and setting the fires. There were laughs, too, trying on all the fancy clothes when the lady visited Edinburgh. The mistress never realised half the things that went on downstairs.

The lady called me in the night before it all happened. 'Irene, can you choose two staff to go up to Carberry? They are in need of help this week.'
'Yes, of course. I'll send Famie and Annie.'
'Must you send Famie?' The lady sighed.
I smiled. 'Annie will keep her right.'
'Yes, but …'
I felt there was something she wasn't telling me.
'Can I ask why they are needing extra help?'
She paused for a second.
'Carberry's lady's sister is visiting with her husband and children, and obviously they need to be prepared.'
'I see.'

I sensed what that meant, and her reluctance to explain why. Even before the King abdicated, whenever the lady's sister visited, someone got sacked. All the staff understood it, and they scanned around, wondering which of them would be let go. They tried to avoid the lady's sister, but she always deemed at least one member of staff required punishing. Maybe it made her feel important, but then, she was married to the king's brother. Now she was the wife of the new king.

Famie and Annie were chosen to help. Both hoped to catch a glimpse of the Royal Family, but Famie appeared worried.
'We'd only get sacked from Carberry,' I heard Annie reassure her as they set off to trudge up the hill. 'Not the big house if she didn't like us. She can't sack us from our main jobs here.'

I later heard about what happened from Famie and Annie, who told the story like this:

Famie and Annie were dusting in the hallway at the bottom of the great stairway. They noticed the princesses playing on the stairs, but they knew not to say anything to them, just get on with their work. The wee one, Margaret, was just six at the time.

Famie was cleaning the bannister, and the next thing she knew, a pair of shoes clattered right down the stairs, just missing her. So, of course, she looked up. There was the wee madam with her hands on her hips, staring at her. Annie was by the suit of armour, so she tucked behind it and watched it all happen.

'Pick up my shoes!' the wee princess shouted to Famie. Famie could see Lilibet watching above. Oh yes, Margaret made sure her sister could see her bossing everyone about. A right 'see what I can do' moment for the wee besom.

Annie couldn't believe it when she heard Famie say, 'No' to the princess, folding her arms to copy the bairn. Famie knew she had deliberately thrown the shoes down the stairs. And, of course, Famie, as obstinate as the wee girl, squared up to her.
Annie whispered to Famie to pick up the shoes. She said, 'Just do it!'

Eventually, Famie gave in and trudged to get them. She needed to work here for the rest of the day. She knew if the lady's sister heard she had defied her child, Famie would be certain for the chop.

Then, all of a sudden, they heard a voice form above shout, 'Stop!'
They all stared up. It was as if God from the heavens had spoken. Lilibet ran up and away, into another room, but Margaret stayed where she was. Famie and Annie were frozen to the spot.
'Don't you ever speak to people like that. Pick them up yourself!' It was the king!
Famie stood still as a statue and watched the wee

girl come down and pick up her shoes. The princess's face was tripping her. The king nodded for Famie to leave, and she and Annie scuttled off.

After I heard Famie and Annie's story, the lady of the house called me in later that day to speak to her. 'I have to let Annie go,' she told me.

Famie had blamed Annie for standing up to the princess, although she had only watched from the side. The wee girl must have run to her mother, and Famie had lied and said Annie was involved. The lady of our house wanted her sacked here, too. I was made to beg to keep her place. If Annie had picked up the shoes when ordered, none of this unpleasantness would have happened, was the thought.

I had spoken to my own mother, who had something up her sleeve, so that Annie was kept on. But it was the end for me and Famie—the absolute end.

The next day, I sent Famie down to the kitchen when I knew it to be empty. Unfortunately, she went down the stairs so hard that I heard that stupid girl's skull crack and her neck twist. I shouted for help, but, of course, I reached her body before anyone else.

'There's been an accident,' I called up to the staff, who appeared at the top of the stairs, standing stock still in horror, their hands over their mouths.

Obviously, she fell. She was a clumsy hulk of a girl. Crouching over her lifeless body, I leant in close, as if to check her pulse. Hoping she might still be in the realm of consciousness, I whispered, 'That's for Donald.'

He was your brother, after all.

All my love,

Irene (Mum) XoX

TWENTY-SEVEN
RHIANNON

JAN and I met up again in a pub along the high street of the town, opposite Debbie's café. Debbie's is closed again, a COVID outbreak. Last time, I'm told, they closed because of complaints made to environmental health. It doesn't half put me off, but Debbie keeps reopening with promises of 'improvements being made to safeguard our customers'.

Kim organised my leaving do in this pub, years ago. For a woman who owned a pub, she spent little time in it, preferring establishments away from her husband's gaze. I think it meant she had freedom to flirt without him watching, an excuse so she could cheat while he worked in the pub.

'I love your shoes! I can't wear heels like you, Rhiannon. I've got to consider weight distribution,' Jan announces, with no build up or introduction. 'I've too much frontage, you see. More front than Blackpool. The boobage and belly mean I'd have to tilt back forty-five degrees or fall flat on my face. I wouldn't walk right one bit.' She revealed a mouthful of white teeth.

I stare at her frontage. I agree she'd tip over. I try to speak, but she goes on too quickly. 'I love your leggings. I prefer Mum jeans. These are great.'

'Oh no, I like the skinny jeans,' I manage to squeeze in.

'That's fine for you, but I remember the 90s, when flares were in, and I was fine. They evened out my big hips. Now, with the skinny jeans and my apple body, I look like Gru from *Despicable Me*. Despicable skinny legs. I look like an orange on a toothpick from the side. It was okay when I was an hourglass, but I've filled out to an apple. I considered a breast reduction, when the rest of me was slimmer, but the rest of my body has caught up, so it's Mum jeans all the way.'

I'm exhausted just listening, but we're a few wines in before Jan finally mentions Kim, unbidden.

'I bumped into Kim on my way here. Oh, what a laugh she is.'

It's obvious she admires Kim and doesn't recall me complaining about her years ago, so I don't fill her in now. She changes the channel.

'Work's done for the week, though. That's good. I'm full time—wears you out. Especially working with grumpy jaws.'

'Who's that?'

'My boss.' She peers about, as if he might lurk behind her. 'I can't say anything in case Kim's sneaked in after me. He's her man.'

'Whose man?'

'Kim! Kim's man!'

'Kim's man is your boss?'

'Yeah, the weirdo.'

I snort. I hope he is a weirdo. 'What a coincidence,' I say, but I am interested now, and I lean in to hear more.

'Rob is anal. I mean, sphincter so tight if he clenched any more, he'd disappear up his own arsehole!' I stifle a giggle as I think, *Rob the knob. This is delightful.*

Kim met him not long after Darren ′passed. Married on the rebound in her grief.'

I doubted that, based on the conversation I remembered from the pub toilet, and the rest of Kim's carry-on with men.

'So, what's he like?'

'English, I think? He was okay to start with. Everyone maintained he was fine enough, but he doesn't speak to anyone now. Looks about ready for a heart attack. A right stress ball of a guy, edgy.'

I nod and let her continue, not wanting this exposé to stop.

'There've been a couple of events where he just totally lost it over nothing. Ready to burst at the slightest thing. He's always short-tempered and overreacting.'

'What like?' I consider Kim's behaviour at work and wonder if she has a twin, although she always seems in control.

'He went mad one day when someone brought in cakes for us and those from my section came over and helped themselves. We were talking, bantering, you know. Nobody said anything. We were just joking about. He went off at them, tipping up the jammie doughnuts.'

'God! He sounds hellish,' I butt in.

'Yeah, I know. I was in the accountants once, and I noticed cuts and bruises on Kim's arm, like when you've been grabbed by somebody. I wondered if he knocked her about.' Jan raises her eyebrows and holds her wine glass in front of her face.

I can't imagine Kim letting that happen, but maybe I have it all wrong. 'Do you think?'

'Dunno. She seems so smiley and friendly, but is it a show? Is she covering up a pile of abuse? It goes to show you never know.'

'He's the head boss, then?' That explained the expensive house in that end of town.

'She landed on her feet with the money situation. She's the manager of the accountants you were at, though, aye?' She has remembered now.

'So she'll have decent money,' I ventured, 'along with the pub money and life insurance she got when Darren died.' The wine is making me brave.

'They have everything—two cars, the best holidays before COVID. She's always dressed up.' Jan puts on a concerned face and voice and whispers, 'but is it worth it all for a life of sadness and bullying?'

'Oh, I don't know ... maybe that is not happening.'

'No, but he looks the type.' She waits, and then nods and announces, with her glass held aloft, 'He has a big dimple on his chin'

'Right.' Is all l can say. I'm confused.

'You ken what that means?'

I shrug.

'I read that means he loves attention. Dimple-chin guys are flirtatious and good at it. I read they're high on affection and sex drive and can get very antsy if they do not have full-time affection of their partners. I reckon she doesn't give him enough, you know.' She winks, and then, after another gulp, carries on with, 'But I don't think he is much to look at.'

I disagree but say nothing.

'And too fat.'

I disagree again to myself, judging him attractive—not that I care.

'Anyway, I wouldn't fancy him on top of me either way, the snake.'

Poor Darren gone, and then this guy pops up straight after. There is something here.

TWENTY-EIGHT

RHIANNON

AFTER JAN LEAVES, I stay on for a bit, checking my phone. No need to hurry home to stare at the wall. I go to the toilets, which remain exactly how they were at my leaving do.

I imagine emerging back out there and the pub being indistinguishable from all those years ago. In my mind, I stepped back into my leaving party.

That's right! I remember how I had spotted a man at the bar. He was well off, smarter that the average guy in there. I didn't recognise him, although I noticed his handsomeness. He kept staring over, so my friend Moya had nudged me. 'He keeps looking at you.'

By then, I was leering at him. He must have been wondering what I was staring at.

Kim gave me the side eye. 'I'll get the drinks. Fling a tenner in the kitty. Write down what you all want.' She threw a used envelope from her bag for us to write on. Within minutes, she shimmied to the bar and stood as close to him as she could.

I sighed. I was leaving anyway; no time to meet handsome at the bar. No point starting up a flirtation in a town I was running from.

But it annoyed me. Kim couldn't notice me wanting anything without wanting it herself.

As soon as she saw I was interested, she felt compelled to make a move. Up at the bar, I watched her stick her bosom out and touch his arm. Later, I stepped out to the toilet near the back door and spied them again—snogging in the alleyway. It reminded me of deja vu. I don't believe in that; it's just neurones in your brain firing off a similar pattern, but I remember how it felt like time travel.

She would have been married to Darren then, but she always took off her wedding ring on nights out.

Heartbroken when he died. My arse.

She was unfaithful the whole marriage—flirting with all the clients, couldn't wait to escape from the bar to the job at the accountants. And then he died, and she married again in no time.

I wonder whether she's faithful to this one. Sounds as if she has met her match, so I'm satisfied. I struggle to remember the face of the man at the bar. I can still envision him: blue eyes, dimpled chin. The dimple-chin guy! But his hair is silver now, not brown. Her association with dimple-chin must have been going on even before Darren died, not after, as Jan had implied.

Dirty scheming bitch. How convenient that Darren ended up out of the way. Did she dispose of him to make way for dimple-chin? Was it for the life insurance, or for the pub she sold straight away? Or am I turning her into a killer in my mind when all I experienced of her was bullying?

I think of the man washing the car—the nice-smelling man with the round cheeks and sharp blue eyes, smiling, waving at the neighbours. Now, dimple-chin might be a wife-beating monster.

What she wanted or what she deserved?

It sparks an idea in my head, something I can't put my finger on.

Something can be done with the knowledge I possess.

PART 2
THE ENDGAME

TWENTY-NINE
ROB

Dear Diary,

I'm writing this down because I can't tell anyone. I wanted to talk to someone, but I felt disloyal, so I started a diary instead.

I'm going to write a story, my story. Everyone at work thinks I'm short-tempered. But it's because I need to keep it all in. If I die, and I believe that could happen, I want everyone to understand what brought about such a situation.

I've left a note on my phone, and this journal in my car. I'm scared she'll find it, because she always checks my messages and emails. She hasn't found the note yet, though. Maybe I'll delete it. Actually, I better do it right away.
I'll write it out and place in my desk drawer at work. If she kills me, when they clear it out, they'll find it. I can't risk her stumbling on it. She knows everything.

I'm not sure where to start, but maybe I need to explain who I am and how I got into this position. One does not end up at my situation by magic, beamed up like in Star Trek. My personality, my childhood upbringing, made me the person I am. Perhaps I'm a perfect type to end up here, with her.

I'm not blaming myself, but others might wonder how I could I allow it. Some might want to comprehend how it grew, how I morphed into the perfect victim. Some might doubt my story entirely, but here it is ...

A long, long time ago, I lived in a small farm outside Edinburgh. As a young child I caught pneumonia, and my lungs collapsed. I spent several days alone in hospital. My lungs were damaged, so I needed daily medication to survive. I missed a lot of schooling, and I couldn't join in with the children tearing around in the playground. On holidays, I'd sit on the beach and watch my brother running on the sand with Dad. I had nothing left to do, so I turned to a shelf full of books in the holiday home. To begin with, I found them difficult to understand, but I kept on. I continued reading when we got home, demanding a library card. By the time I was eight, I could devour novels at teenage level and higher.

At school, I was weak and clever, so almost inevitably I became a target for bullies. In the late 1970s, bullying was part of growing up, normal. For years, I was ridiculed, shoved around by those who were stronger and stupider. I was too scared to tell anyone, so I developed the ability to 'grin and bear it'. Pack the pain down deep inside. Pretend it was not happening. I thought I was being strong, manly. I was strong on the outside and silent. However, I loved the airy-fairy world of make believe. I preferred the dream state of books, where I could disappear into another world. Those worlds existed only in my mind. A world where I wasn't bullied, where I felt popular, where people were kind. My fantasy world was better than the real one. It became my way of coping.

At twelve, almost without warning, my lungs repaired and, like any ill person who becomes well again, I revelled in my health and strength. Instead of taking the school bus, I ran. I hiked for miles and did press-ups just because I could. I felt physically strong, like a man should, as well as strong enough to cover up my feelings. I honestly believed my positive thoughts and dreams had made the difference. I figured I had conjured up my own healing in my head. I joined a karate club and excelled at it.

I got a job in the corner shop as a paper boy, sweeping up. Kimberly, aged fifteen, a few years older than me, served there. I had more in common with the younger children, as I missed out on all the running and chasing earlier. I suppose I was immature, young for my age. Still, I suppose Kimberly became my first girlfriend.

Then my father died. After a few years, mother sold the farm and moved my brothers and me to England, with her new husband. The man treated me well, and I led a happy life there. I was far from the weakling of my youth. Far from the place of my youth, too. I grew strong, physical, and confident. For a while, I experimented with art, music, and more reading about how to expand my mind, although I mainly felt comfortable in the mainstream, sticking to the rules.

I was popular. I had numerous girlfriends. Sometimes, anxiety crept over me, and the insecure child inside sneaked out, but the breathing exercises I learnt as a child helped me cope with any developing panic attacks. The amazing control I had over my body gave me the ability to fight and the mental power to win. And always on the surface all looked well. I kept it all in, all well hidden to be the man I was meant to be. I made it to college, and then got a well-paid job in sales.

The real changes took place after I moved north again. Mother had returned there after her second husband died. She married again and moved into the town close to the farm where we lived when I was a child. It was there that I met Kimberly again.

THIRTY

RHIANNON

 I'd tried to reinvent myself at university, to make improvements. If everyone at home said I was 'up myself', I decided to head right up there. I couldn't wait to escape to university, to the place where I fitted in, where I thought I could present myself as someone else. Of course, my past kept seeping through: my patterns of speech, my experiences. How I'd grown up still showed.

I was superior to everyone back home, but at university? I wasn't clever enough. I was caught between two worlds, neither of which I belonged to. I didn't even understand who I was, which depended on who I talked to at the time. I wanted people to admire me so much I'd mimic whoever's company I kept. A chameleon. I could always relate to people with different backgrounds. I'd disguise myself with a mask, a costume. I'd copy ways of speech, but putting up a front tired me out. In the main, my act caused me to be well thought of, but sometimes I'd stick in a phase, like a chameleon changing colour halfway, as if startled. The

*facade presented itself. Sometimes, a trip-up occurred.
I'd freeze when a predator noticed.*

*I don't feel bad about it. A lot of people adapt to
their environment. You don't tell a dirty joke to the bank
manager when going for a loan. You don't talk slang to
the middle-class English couple on holiday. Geoff and
Sandra from Stoke-on-Trent wouldn't appreciate the
incredible Scottish compliment of being called 'good
c*nts.'*

*When I returned to work with Kim after university,
she was already married to Darren. The wedding was
news to me, although I'd known they were engaged, of
course. I wasn't invited to the do. I'd lost contact, having
the time of my life at university. I used home as a base in
the holidays to head into an Edinburgh office job. I was
in commuter-ville before it was normal around here.*

*I never socialised in the village if I could avoid it.
When I did venture out there, it never went well.*

*I was in my twenties when we took in a night out at
the bowling club. Even if I didn't possess delusions of
grandeur, my relatives did on my behalf. We sat with the
local gay guy, the hairdresser, Gordon. Later, he was
known as Gay Gordon, when such things became open.
His sexuality was not referred to in public; it was a wink
and a nod. 'He's good to his mother.'*

*He suggested I dance with a young lad who was
hanging around. I made to stand up, but Auntie Nettie
pulled me back down. 'I don't think so. You're not going
with that rubbish,' she announced.*

'Oi! That's my cousin's laddie,' Gordon protested.

*'No' good enough for her.' My auntie put her foot
down.*

Gordon frowned. 'Oh aye, what's so great about her?'

He looked me up and down. 'I ken her mother and father from the crescent.'

'She went away to university to get away from that trash.' She cackled a hearty cigarette-induced wheeze. She meant it as a joke. 'She is too clever for all of you lot.' She threw her arm around to indicate the whole bar.

'Well, she should stay away then.' Gordon took her seriously.

I wanted to protest, but I sat there taking it all in, never uttering a word.

'If we're not good enough for you, what you doing here?'

'I'm just having night out,' I pleaded.

'Tourist, are you?' He snorted.

'No, sorry. I'll dance with him.' I scanned the room. He had wandered away.

'Sit doon!' Auntie grabbed my arm and pushed me back in my seat.

Gordon screwed up his face, about to speak.

Aunt Nettie leant forward. 'Fuck you, and fuck the lot of you!' Nettie cackled to the whole room. Gordon giggled too.

I'd never felt so uncomfortable in my life.

After that, I took a room in a flat in Easter Road to stay near the office in Edinburgh in the holidays, rather than go home at all. I returned sporadically, but never to the village. Though Mum kept referring to 'your room' at Great-granny Irene's house, I never slept in it again after the age of eighteen.

THIRTY-ONE
ROB

Dear Diary,

I met her in the local pub, the week after I'd returned up north. She was married, but she had split up with her husband. I spotted straightaway that she was not wearing a ring. She told me they were over in all but name, so we started seeing each other. They hadn't been getting on for years, she claimed. Still, it was tragic for her when he died three months into our dating.

I met up with her the day she found out. She told me she needed me to help her recover from the tragedy. I felt so much for her—sympathy, mostly, I guess. It was early days, and there was no basis to form love, but empathy is my strong point. I sense others pain more than my own. The depth of feeling I felt for her had to be love, right?

We enjoyed an exciting relationship and a whole lot of fun together. Then the emotional abuse started. She allowed me to go to work, but my travel to and from work was monitored. She insisted I call her in my lunch break.

I tried to split up with her when this started, but she blackmailed me, threatening to overdose on tablets if left. I was optimistic, still thinking things could improve between us. I moved in with her after a year. I thought this would make her more settled, more secure. It was an enormous mistake. Things spiralled rapidly downwards from then.

The first attack happened in a supermarket when we disagreed on what to buy for dinner. She froze, and I noticed her reddening, then she wandered over to me, smiling, and kicked me right in the shins. It happened without warning, in the empty aisle.
'Okay. Well get what you want,' she sang when a lady wandered around the corner. It was as if it never happened. That one act from her caused a crack in the confidence I had built up. I could hardly retaliate. What would people think?

Other times, she stood on my toes hard, then flipped to smiling and being kind as soon as anyone looked. Severe yet subtle. It all occurred in secret, yet in full view.

The following month, one Friday night after dinner, a vicious attack occurred. I left the door open, as I had bags to carry in, things she had demanded I pick up on my way home. I forgot to go back and shut the door, and I heard her slam it hard. She flew towards me and grabbed my nipples, twisting them as hard as possible. It was such a bizarre, agonising occurrence. It shocked me to my core.

She turned on the TV, as if nothing had happened. Kim was able to switch from normal to untamed in an instant.

The violence heightened. The next time she attacked me, she chased me around the house, slapping me on the head, smacking me with a broom she had picked up on the way. I fell to the floor, but she leant over me, whacking with both hands until she wore herself out. She beat me in such a savage manner that I couldn't believe it happened. I became detached, watching it from above, like I could my bullying at school. I was able to suffer it, and blot it out, to act as if all was normal.

She bruised her hand one time, she hit me so hard. Evidence existed that time. Usually, we pretended nothing had happened.
'Ow,' she winced as she opened the fridge door.
'Are you okay?'
'Yeah. My hand is sore.'
'Yes,' I replied. We both knew why.
She shifted on her feet and said, 'If only you'd try to improve yourself.'
At least she acknowledged I had been involved, but in her mind, the bruising was my fault.

I started reading again, lots of books and daydreaming about my perfect girlfriend, believing I could manifest everything. It would be all right.

THIRTY-TWO

RHIANNON

WHEN KIM GOT FED up with the landlady gig in the pub and took the manager's job where I eventually worked, she got it based on her managerial skills at the pub. She got herself promoted above her qualifications, of which she had none, but she looked the part and dealt with the public well.

On Kim's thirtieth birthday, we all gathered in the reception, ready to head out for drinks.

'You're thirty too, right?' she said to me with a smile. Her minion seemed shocked and opened her mouth to speak. Kim glared a warning before returning her stare to me, her head slightly cocked. She was thirty, and she knew damn well I was twenty-four. She knew me from the village. She was my babysitter. *How the hell would that work if we were the same age?*

'No.'

'Really?' She threw me a sickening grin. 'Are you sure?'

I couldn't answer. I felt my face boil, the heat creeping up my neck.

'I thought you were.' She shrugged, sticking her bottom lip out as she tried to stifle a smile. Her wee friend giggled at her rudeness. A knock came from the recently locked door.

'Get that,' Kim barked.

Moya opened the door and returned after a few seconds.

'Ooh, a delivery!' Kim grabbed the flowers. Her face lit up as she eagerly opened the card, but then, like turning off a light, all the colour drained from her face. She paused. 'Oh, they are for you.' She glanced up from the card. 'From Mr B.'

'I thought he fancied you, Kim,' stated Moya.

Kim threw her a dry stare. 'Shut up, Moya.' She turned to me. 'You realise it's not ethical to have relationships with clients?'

'It's just flowers. A thank-you.'

'Aye, right. What did you do to get those?' She nodded at the boss, who appeared concerned.

I faced him. 'A thank you.' I felt I needed to explain.

'Mm-hmm,' was the only noise that emanated from Kim.

As we left, I noticed her slip off her wedding ring and sneak it into a compartment in her bag. She marched in front of me, rigid and upright, like a soldier on parade. She carried her bag straight at her left side, her right hand holding a gift bag she had been given. She didn't swing her arms as she walked. She reminded me of an Irish dancer in her movements.

I kept my gift for the pub. I had decided to kill her with kindness, maybe then she might let up.

Preston arrived as we exchanged gifts. As I passed my gift over, Kim's face froze. I could tell she was still stony with embarrassment and fury over the incident with the flowers.

'Hiya!' Preston sang.

'Hello, you!' She grinned.

'Happy Birthday, you old trout.' He grinned, and Kim threw her head back, laughing. Was throwing insults a way to suck up to her? 'Hurry up and open the presents. I've folk waiting,' Preston carried on.

I handed over my gift of expensive perfume.

'Preston, the taxi is here,' his friend shouted from the door.

'Ooh,' cooed Moya as Kim pulled my gift half out the bag. Moya leant into Kim so she could peer in better. Kim gave it a cursory glance before putting it back in the bag and moving to the other gifts.

'Fine, aye,' was all she uttered.

'Preston!' shouted his friend again from the door. 'Come on!'

Preston yelled back, 'I'm coming! Bye everyone.' As he left, he whispered in my ear,

'Oh my God, what did you give her? A shite in a bag?'

THIRTY-THREE
ROB

Dear Diary,

No one can explain why people stay with an abusive partner, but I did. Over the years, I suffered beatings several times a month at her hand. Nightly, I'd balance on a tightrope of anger and anxious appeasement, trying to keep things level, calm, tolerating jibes, keeping the conversation pleasant until she passed out asleep. I'd tread on eggshells for five hours every evening on workdays, and the whole of the weekend.

On top of this, I endured the embarrassment of explaining the black eyes and the bruises at work. My strong build caused people to judge me unlikely to be bossed around, and perhaps, if attacked, able to tolerate it.

With my training in karate, I could have fought her off, but I did not want to hurt someone I loved. It's a basic component of love, not allowing anything to harm the object of your affections. It would almost be like harming oneself. And what kind of man hits a woman anyway? It was not even possible for me to consider.

I wanted to be a loving husband, even if that did not resonate with her.

I'm not saying I'm perfect. I was selfish too. I raised her above my own needs, only because I wanted her love in return.

The daily dismissal of my efforts caused my love to dwindle, since it was not being reciprocated. My love was not unconditional. I gave love because I wanted to receive love. I gave love, and she took it—a different dynamic.

I used to do everything I could for her with nothing in return. I paid for everything. I understand that's the man's role, but she ran up debts without any consideration. But I soon learnt that I also paid in other ways, and that nothing I did would ever be enough.

THIRTY-FOUR

RHIANNON

 I tried to ignore her, but that resulted in her upping her game to provoke a reaction. She wanted revenge on me for having the audacity to leave the village. Who did I think I was? There was hardly any pride for someone who'd done well, bettered themselves, got a business or made more money. Instead, jealousy or envy knifes the gut of those who couldn't or wouldn't do better.

Her manager's job increased her status, but that paled into insignificance when I, a kid from the next street, attended university. It diminished her high opinion of herself. I had positioned myself above her in the pecking order, but as management, she controlled my day. She could—and did—make my life difficult. She would not help or assist me but instead would trip me up, put obstacles in my way, and cause me grief.

Then there were her comments. I mentioned the blouses the others wore, all pretty and matching. She commented she'd arrange one for me.

'I guess a size sixteen?' she said. *Two sizes bigger than I was.*

'Twelve,' I replied.

She snorted and raised an eyebrow at her friend. 'Fine ... if you say so.' She eyed me from head to toe. 'But we do prefer if you have it ironed for work.'

I pulled my cardigan over my crumpled blouse; hers was immaculately pressed.

'Right, okay.' There was no point arguing.

'I like to iron my things for work. It doesn't take long. I think it appears professional. Maybe you could do it while you are watching TV. What do you do, Stacey?'

'Yeah, I do mine at the weekend, when the boys are at football.'

'I did iron it. It just got a bit ...' I protested, but Kim interrupted. 'I'm not saying you didn't iron it. I'm saying it doesn't look like you did,' she sniggered, rolling her eyes at her buddy.

Why do people do that? Do they believe you can't notice them pull faces at you right in front of them? I saw it, and remember it now with the same anger.

Why am I going over all this? I give myself a headache. This isn't healthy. I'm going to forget all about her again.

THIRTY-FIVE

ROB

Dear Diary,

She paused, and then turned and backhanded me hard in the face. I stood and stared. I'd only asked her how her day had been. I racked my brain for an explanation, but I couldn't find one.

'What? Why?' I whined.
She sneered. 'You get on my nerves. You're so perfect.'
I pulled my hand away from my face, considering it. Everyone does that when they're in pain; they check for blood. It hurts, so there must be blood. I saw no evidence of any, despite the stinging.

'Sorry.' She slid towards me with a pout, but no sorrow or pity in her eyes.
'Sorry,' she repeated in a sing-song voice. Her smile took the sting out somewhat, as her happiness meant another slap didn't seem likely. I preferred her mockery to her rage.
Blinking, I said, 'You can't do that, for goodness sake. What if I did

that to you?' I was stronger then, still able to stand up for myself. Only later did I learn not to argue back.

Her brow furrowed at my defiance. 'I won't do it again,' she said, matter-of-factly.

'How do I know that?' I stepped into the bathroom to witness the redness in my face, fading already. It wasn't too hard of a slap, but she had inflicted it for nothing at all. Before, there had always been a trigger, however small.

I packed to leave, prepared myself for the firing line downstairs. I felt a pang of disappointment that Kim had already left with the dog. Sullen, I drove to my mother's house, my heart heavy. I couldn't even turn the radio on; it made too joyful a sound.

'I've left her,' I announced, as I marched down the hall past the open kitchen door. The back door was always open.

'What happened?' Mum was drying her hands on a tea towel.

'We had an argument.' I couldn't bring myself to explain the rest, and by now there were no marks on my face as evidence. She wasn't so strong as to leave a lasting impression.

'Well, in the morning you'll need to go back. Couples argue. Have you been giving her enough attention?'

'What?'

'You men! You never realise when women are telling you things are wrong, not until they explode. She has probably been telling you for weeks things aren't going well.' She glanced at my stepfather, behind the paper, and sighed. 'I sometimes think men don't hear women at all. Their voices are too high, like the opposite of Alsatians and those whistles that only they can hear.'

To prove her right, I stopped listening. I reasoned I might have taught Kim a lesson by walking out. If she did it again, I might leave forever.

'Oh, you're back. Super. Great timing. I prepared dinner,' Kim sang on *my arrival home. She'd cooked enough for two. There must have been no doubt in her mind that I would be back.*

I believe the only thing she ever loved was the dog. I say loved, but perhaps it was that she felt content with the dog. It was a being she controlled fully, with no chance of rebellion. She had ailurophobia. I searched up the proper name for the phobia of cats. She hated cats. So did Hitler, Napoleon, Mussolini, Julius Caesar and Genghis Khan, so she joined esteemed company.

Knowing what I now know, I often judge people who aren't animal people, especially the 'not cat' ones. When she wanted a dog, it had to be a boxer or a terrier. People like Kim love to control animals, as they do people. Dogs are submissive, almost cowardly. Dogs beg for attention. Kim loved that.

I owned a cat when I met Kim; it never bothered her for months, until one day she turned up her nose at it and insisted I put it out or lock it up. She claimed she could smell cat as soon as she entered the house. She refused to sit on the furniture for all the hairs. She maintained she was allergic, but she never developed a rash or sneezed.

One night, we went out for dinner and returned home. The cat bounded across the fence and we heard a car careening too fast, a screech, and a tha-thump. I realised what had happened right away. Unable to view the scene, I ran into the house. Kim came in soon after. 'Is the ... the cat ... is he okay?'

'No, it's dead. The woman who knocked him down wants to speak to you.'

I shook my head. 'No, I ... I can't! I can't ... speak.' The words stumbled out of my mouth. I struggled to catch a breath, and tears welled in my eyes.

'Come on. She's waiting outside. She is upset. She wants to apologise.'

'No.'

'What? the poor woman is upset. I told her you'd come out.'

'I'm upset.'

'For God's sake, it's just a cat,' she bit.

'Can you tell her I understand it was an accident. I can't face anyone right now.'

'Fine. I'm going to look stupid now, but fine.' She stormed out. She returned carrying a cardboard box.

What is wrong with you? That was so embarrassing. She just wanted to apologise, and you can't even have the decency to do that.'

'I could not speak to her.'

'Rude!'

'I couldn't. I didn't want to her to see me in this mess.'

'Pathetic. You have disappointed me today, Robert.'

'I couldn't see anyone. I got a shock.'

'I don't care. You were plain ignorant. What will she think?'

'I was in a state.' I opened my eyes to her showing me the cat in box. I glimpsed in, but couldn't bear it.

Kim shook her head and glanced in too. She screwed up her face, left the cat there at my feet, and slammed the door on her exit.

She didn't speak to me for three days. When she returned, she said she needed to teach me a lesson about how to treat people.

A few weeks later, she told a story of a man at work. 'He was acting funny, so I asked what's wrong? He had tears in his eyes, and he said, "My cat. I've had to take him to the vets to get him put down." Aw, I thought, how sweet and soft-hearted he must be. Bless.'

I felt perturbed. She had no sympathy when my cat died, but she spoke with understanding about the man at work. However, she had performed that particular act of empathy in front of all the staff. She was showing compassion to an audience.

There were never any witnesses to observe her cruelty to me.

THIRTY-SIX

RHIANNON

 I can't forget about her. I try to, but the more I try, the more she's on my mind. It is the very definition of temptation.

On a diet, I crave food more that when I am not. It turns into all I obsess about.

Today, I wandered by her workplace, but Kim was nowhere to be seen. I left it for a while, and then started checking her out on social media. We had lots of mutual friends, so I could access snippets of what she posted if they commented, much of it not private. I scrolled through photos of her with dimple-chin man, smiling out as if they were the happiest couple in the world.

I peered at her all-smiling Facebook page. She appeared unchanged. I knew I didn't. I look older than her now. Kim must experience no stress, no guilt. She is mean, nasty, horrible—and radiant.

It must be great to feel guilt-free. Guilt can show in your face. Calm people appear well lifelong, like blameless Christians or meditative hippies, or psychopaths. I knew she was fifty-five, but she could pass for ten years younger. I'm not quite fifty, and someone has already asked if I've retired. A sixty-year-old lady at church imagined I must be her age. She argued with me about it, as if I'd forgotten my own birthdate. Perhaps she believed I had dementia, since I appear so elderly, the daft boot.

Kim dresses well. Being a bitch looks fine. How can she look so well on it? Her new husband was better looking than her last. When the anniversary of Darren's death came around, her friends had posted pictures on social media. Even so long ago, Darren appeared worn. This couple, in contrast, were shiny, smiling, beaming pictures of health. Kim's cheeks were plump and glowing, her hair preened, and her clothes fresh and ironed. I could almost smell the expensive perfume I'd bought for her, and I knew his aftershave was bound to be vibrant.

I'm thinner than her, but I'm drawn. Mum always tells me to fatten up.

'You need a bit of timbre when you are older. There are no wrinkles in a blown-up balloon,' she'd say. Clearly, I'm a deflated one.

THIRTY-SEVEN
RHIANNON

KIM'S FACEBOOK shows her out at dinner with a friend. She'd commented about her pal, in a photo of them at a local restaurant. Her friend isn't on Facebook it seems, but Kim has named her, so I'm certain of who she is.

I was reminded of a time when Kim twirled a pen in front of me and told me to head off to work at another branch. She'd smiled, but her eyes said something else. *Did I hear a cackle of a laugh?* Maybe I invented that.

At the other branch, the manager who had arranged me coming over, Sheona McPherson, was not at work, as it was a Saturday morning and she worked during the week. I worked half a day. Though fine enough, the staff weren't friendly; rather, they were all over the male colleague I started with, but that's women sometimes. I thought to myself, *Head down and on with the job.*

I attended to a number of clients and worked the way I always did. They gave me no particular guidance or instruction.

Sheona called me on the Monday, with no pleasantries to start the conversation.

'I have heard reports of your behaviour and have had to call you about it.'

'Okay,' I replied, dragging it out.

'I've had it reported to me that you did not record the necessary details on the files all day.'

'Oh, I' m sorry. I didn't realise there was more to record.'

'There are parts missing. I need to express my concern over this and let you know you must not do this.'

'Okay, I misunderstood what we were to record. I did have all the necessary conversations, but if the client answered no, I didn't record them.'

'I'd rather you record the question, and even if not confirmed and negative replies given, still record them. Then I can see you have at least asked the questions. To be clear, you must also write down that the client said no.'

'Okay. I haven't done it that way before.'

'Well, you must do it that way here.'

I decided not to argue.

'Okay, no problem. Is that it?'

'You're saying okay. You will do this in the future?'

'Yes, of course. I guess that is what you want. I will record things the way you want.'

I felt quite disappointed. It was not the welcome I'd hoped for, but I considered that the end of the discussion. I was about to say goodbye and hang up; however, she carried on. 'Oh, well ... and other things ...'

'Oh?'

'I heard you were unpleasant to the staff.'

'Pardon?'

'You came in and didn't introduce yourself.'

'I did.'

'Not what I heard.'

'I'm sorry. I thought this call was about the way I recorded things, not how I was with the staff.' I felt provoked. It felt like a telling off.

THIRTY-EIGHT

RHIANNON

WHAT DOES it feel like to be lonely? It feels like hunger while everyone around you prepares for a meal. It hurts as hunger pangs hurt, but it resembles malnutrition—the lack of something needed to survive.

I stick to regular routines. I work and I sleep. I read. I focus on work because it's a reliable set-up that never changes. It comforts me; it cannot surprise me. The fact that I love my job is dangerous, because loneliness gives me space to work further, perpetuating and justifying the situation.

Most of the time, I am okay with this. I'm not unhappy. Solitude gives me time to think, however, which is all I can do—that and read, write in my notebook, or continue reading the letters from that box of Mum's. It's strange to see your ancestors in a different light, to hear things they never talked about at Christmas or around the table.

I put a frozen pizza in the oven, too lazy to prepare anything fancy. As I wait, I can't help but run over all Kim's misdemeanours, testing my brain to recall everything in detail, until I'm tired so I lie on the couch in a trance, visualising it all.

I smelt gas one morning, when I arrived before everyone else, so I quickly phoned the gas board. When Kim arrived, she declared, 'You had no right to do that!' She rolled her eyes at the followers who had come in after her.

'I thought it was the best thing to do,' I replied.

'I can't smell gas. Can you smell gas, Moya?' she asked, glaring at me all the while.

'No,' whispered Moya, shaking her head.

'No one can,' Kim announced, surrounded by all the staff who wanted to watch the show. And then to her audience, she added, 'Just her, who thinks it's her job to manage this place.'

I left, humiliated, and shut myself in my office. Kim called to cancel the gas board. Then the boss turned up and called the gas board because he smelt gas. Kim would have rather have us all blown up than let me take charge of anything.

I demanded thirty-minute meeting times; she decreased them to twenty minutes, so I ran into lunch times.

I grind my teeth thinking about it, but I'm tired and slip into a dream state.

I dream about the leaving do, the birthday party. Then the fire drifts in. I can smell the smoke. Something clears in my vision. The village floats in fog, and when I approach closely, my eyes adjust so I can focus. It is a faded image: a shadowy, upright figure. I'm getting nearer something.

I wake to the smoke alarm going off. I flap at it with a cushion and open the kitchen door to smoke pouring out of the oven.

The stupid effing pizza resembles a crisp, black Frisbee.

THIRTY-NINE

RHIANNON

I OPEN the local paper over coffee to see Mum right there on page 3. It's not one of *those* papers—she's fully clothed, thank goodness. It's an article titled 'In Their Own Words', which the local rag has run interviewing some of the village's elderly residents about their recollections for International Celebrate our Elders Week.

I sniff at the thought that no one asked me whether it was okay to interview her. *A dangerous game. Half of them are potty and can't even remember their own names, let alone anything else. They're probably all made-up stories.*

I think about complaining to Lesley at the home. I'm Mum's power of attorney, after all. Who knows what nonsense Mum might have come up with? If she's mentioned Ronnie Corbett and Billy Connolly asking her out, I'm going to freak.

I straighten the page and begin to read the article under Mum's photograph.

IN 1968, I got married to a boy from outside the village, David. He was Catholic, so I changed religion for him. That was a huge deal for my family, but my grandmother Marie had the last word, as always. 'Write your own script,' she said.

My wee girls were born in the early 1970s: Rhiannon, and then Jocelyn. Oh, I got some stick in the village for those names.

'Is no one called Jean and Mary these days?' they complained, but I thought them modern-sounding, and I fancied them.

We'd still enjoy the weekend trip to Blackpool in September every year, which Granny Marie arranged, but with extra money, we could afford to book a week away in the summer too. We took the girls to Butlin's holiday camp in the annual trades holidays, which all the men got off work. Most of the village emptied to do the same. We'd meet our neighbours from across the way in chalets, like we were at home.

Even the neighbours travelled. They hated me for some reason, but they and their four snotty-nosed children turned up on the bus from St Andrew's Square with us.

Mum huffed when she saw them and said something about women who'd let men 'have a go' for a bag of tatties, but I didn't know what that meant at the time. They travelled with empty cases to Butlin's, but they always returned home with full ones. They'd swipe anything they could that wasn't nailed down. She always turned up with a massive bag at mealtimes. They owned a whole dinner service nicked from the dining room, bit by bit—a fork one day, a cup the next. Their kitchen cupboards were full of tiny jars of jam.

'Hooray!' we all shouted, as the servers, balancing trays laden with ten plates, shimmied up and down the aisles, serving what seemed like an arena full of people all at once. They served oxtail soup, meat and two veg, and then custard (with a skin on, if you were last served). One server shimmied too fast and a set of plates crashed to the ground, to another cheer. The neighbour helped herself to whatever she could during the distraction.

I caught her once in a photo. The official photographer always took a picture of the crowd, during the evening's entertainment. There she was, sitting behind me, eyeing up my cardigan, which I'd placed on the back of my seat in the Stuart ballroom. I never saw it again. I was too busy watching the knobbly knees contest.

My husband, David, would head off to the Pig and Whistle pub and leave me dancing with the bairns in the huge hall. All the men did that, and we'd find them later, in the smoke and lager-scented crowd, when they forgot to come and join us later on. Maureen disappeared off to put her bairns to bed, returning in no time.

'What're you doing back? What about the bairns?' I asked.

'What's it to do with you, ginger?' She brushed off my concerns with a shrug, and said, 'They're in the chalet just fine.'

'Will you not need to check on them?

'No, they're asleep.'

'I'll go check on them.' I got up to leave.

'Ach, leave them there. The redcoats will let

me know if there a bairn crying in the chalets. I'm out for a good time'.

I glared at her. 'You can't do that,' I declared.

'I can! Everybody does. That's why they have folk patrolling up and down, listening for bairns greeting. They put a sign up if there's one playing up.' She gave me a dirty look as she got up. 'I'm away to the Beachcomber Bar. Come on, Jenny.'

'What about your husband?'

'What about him?' She laughed.

'Well, I'm away with mine to bed,' I announced, as she waltzed down the stairs with Jenny.

David didn't come back to the chalet, so I took a chance as the bairns lay asleep. I knocked up on my Granny Irene's door in the chalet next door, to keep an eye on them. Then I headed to the Pig and Whistle.

I found Alec there. I didn't want to speak to him, but I had no choice. 'Hey, where's Davy?'

He glared at me. 'I dinnae ken,' he grunted, turning his back.

I ventured out again, tugging my jacket around me—summer in Scotland needs a jacket, even in July—and headed to the ballroom. I could hear laughter from the Beachcomber Bar. I hated it in there. It was all slappers and drunks. I spotted Jenny with a redcoat called Ian.

'Have you seen Davy?'

'Aye, he was here earlier.'

I glanced about for Maureen, but I couldn't catch her either. Giving up, I wandered back down to the play park and cable cars, a hive of activity during the day, but quiet this late. I heard a noise, some giggling.

Peering around the corner, my arms folded, I followed the noise to find David pushed against the neighbour, whose knickers were at her ankles. I grabbed his hair.

'Oh, ya!' he yelled, as I slapped him over and over.

Maureen slid down the wall and crumpled in a heap. David had to pull me off her in case I strangled her then and there.

I wrestled free, but not before he was left standing there, holding my jacket. I stood there for a minute, my hands on my hips and my thumbs digging into my back so I felt something sharper than anger. Then I turned and ran to tell Granny, but not until I walked several laps of the camp to calm down. I never saw that jacket again either.

I remember the fire that got Maureen and those poor bairns in the end, too. The smell. The heat. They were all in there at the time, although Alec ran out. The eldest, Kimberly, watched with my daughter Rhiannon. She didn't cry. Didn't seem happy or sad. All those poor wee bairns.

We watched from across the road as the men tried to enter the blaze to help, all beaten back by the flames and smoke. Maybe it was an accident. Alec always did keep his power tools in the kitchen. But there was always this nagging suspicion.

. . .

JESUS, *Mum! It must have been a slow news day*, I think, surprised they'd even print such a thing and worried about defamation. *Did they even read it before they printed it?* But I guess Maureen and Alec are no longer around to challenge it. Kim's elderly dad passed away with COVID-19 during the first lockdown, shortly after receiving his telegram from the Queen.

I'm definitely speaking to Lesley.

FORTY
ROB

Dear Diary,

She lightened up for a while, planning the wedding. I reasoned that, if we married, she might settle. I guessed her controlling ways were caused by her insecurities. She was scared I'd leave. The wedding vows would show her I would stay.

We booked a weekend away. When we stopped off for a lunch on the way back, she complained about the service and refused to pay the bill. She wanted me to back her up, wanted me to tell the café manager that her place was a dump. But I refused.

As she vented to the staff, I paid the bill and got into the car, leaving her to carry on. When she got in the car, she lashed out biting me and scratching.

I grabbed her wrists. 'That's not going to happen again. I refuse to stand by and let this continue.'
She justified her outburst by telling me about her troubled childhood,

without love or affection, without stability or continuity—and I bought it.

'I'm marrying you. I'm your continuity,' I announced. I thought, I can be her saviour! as she fell into my arms. I hoped to help her, to prove men could be caring and considerate. It didn't occur to me that she was acting it all out, an award-level show.

She was skilled at appearing broken. My mistake was in thinking I could help her.

I was a willing participant. I had someone who always needed me. She needed me to hand her the power to abuse. I made a life out of enabling a professional bully who wanted to imprison me within our mutual dependency.

The first months of our marriage were the best period we enjoyed together. We loved each other's company. It felt rewarding and, as we grew closer, we became more interdependent. However, when I pursued promotion, she became irritated. She hadn't known I had gone for the interview, so she developed something against it. It meant more money for us, but she maintained she hated change.

'Turn it down,' she demanded. When I refused, she hit me for the first time in our married life. I harboured the hope this was only a blip, but deep down, I sensed a pattern.

'You can't be hungry,' she would insist, as if I lied about wanting a snack purely to annoy her. Even my belly rumbling became a personal insult.

'No, I'm probably not hungry,' I'd eventually agree. It was easier to agree, and maybe she was right. She turned my feelings into questions. All of my reactions were likely wrong. I doubted my hunger, my thirst, even my temperature.

'I'm boiling.'

'You can't be hot.'

'Okay, I'm not.' But the sweat dripping down my forehead told otherwise. Kim overrode everything until even the physiological workings of my body were incorrect.

We spent time together at the gym in high summer. I forked out a hefty sum for monthly memberships. She demanded the most expensive club, despite it being on the far side of the city and despite me remembering that the sun blinded me through the floor to ceiling windows there.

After finishing our workout and taking showers, we met in the foyer. I waited on her, as men often do with ladies. Then I realised I hadn't drunk enough in in this heat.
'I'm thirsty, Kim. I need some water.' I sauntered to the drinks machine, but searching my pockets, found I had no change. 'Have you got change for the machine?' I asked her.
She glanced at me sideways. 'What for? Water? I'm not paying for water! You should have drunk in the gym. It's free from the cooler. Is there a cooler here?'
'No. There's only bottles from the machine. Have you got change?'
'You don't need water.'
'It's a pound, Kim.'
'Wait until we're home.' She indicated that was the end of the matter.
'I'm really thirsty. Sandpaper mouth.' I pointed to my tongue and chuckled.
She pulled her purse out of her bag, but then spun to face the receptionist and booked a facial for next week. When she opened her purse for her card, I spotted the coins. All I needed was a single pound coin. She paid for her facial in advance with our joint account card.

I considered just taking the purse for a second, but she not only held the purse, she held the power. Plus, the assistant might have thought me rude or bullying. Perhaps she would think I was the controlling one.

She couldn't spare me the pound, because my discomfort meant nothing to her. 'I'd do anything for you' had become 'I'll do nothing for you', or even 'If it adds to your misery, I'll rub it in.'
'I'm really thirsty, Kim,' I reminded her.
'Stop whining. We'll be home soon.' She made for the door.

She drove me home, but not before she dropped a gift off at a friend's house and stopped for petrol. I eyed the drinks on the counter from the car, hoping she might relent and surprise me with one. 'I'll just pop in a minute to work. I forgot a bit of paperwork,' she added. Once there, she stood speaking to the man next door for a while.

In all, it took us two hours to get home. Upset by then, my thirst bunched tight in my chest. I gulped down a jug of water as soon as I got in the door.
'Do you have to gulp so noisily?'
My need for life-giving fluid irritated her, but this time, she did not hit me, which disturbed me. What was coming next?

She stood in front of me and slid off her dressing gown, posing naked.
'Hello, there.' I perked up with a smile and a raised eyebrow. Then she started beating herself with her hairbrush, scratching herself, screaming, 'Stop it! Ow! That hurts!'
I stood in front of her, frozen and confused. 'What's all this about?'

She continued to smile as she finished her assault. Then she tugged her bathrobe back on and pulled a dictator from her pocket.
'What's that?'
'My back-up plan. It's a game, you see, like chess.' She sniffed as she left the room. 'If you say anything about me, I'll prove you did it all along.'

People must have seen her bruises the next day. I could see them standing out, but then, I knew they were there. I'd seen them the night before. 'Can't you cover them up with makeup' I suggested when she was getting ready for work. She seemed appalled. 'No, I think I'll leave them as they are.'
It's just that folk might think I did it.'
She shrugged.

I hoped people would not believe the lies, but I knew some people always believe the worst. The bigger the lie, the more people will believe it.

Kim sighed and tied her scarf, and then, picking up her bag hurried off to work. 'Obviously, you'll need to change your behaviour, or people will realise what you're really like one day,' she said.
'Oh, Kim.'
Her nostrils flared as she stared at me for a second. I winced, ready for the blow. Then she opened the door, and announced, 'The evidence is there. Check.'

FORTY-ONE

RHIANNON

MY VISIT to the home is uneventful. Lesley points out that Mum was lucid enough to sign the consent form and says I should take it up with the journalist if I have any problem.

Mum jabbers on with some story about how she met the woman opposite and her son seems like a lovely boy.

'He got me a biscuit when he went to get his Mum one. About your age,' she hints.

Hardly a boy then, Mum, I muse. *Sure, I'll marry this guy and live happily ever after. It's as easy as that. Make sure to let him in on your plan.*

'Now about those letters,' Mum taps the wooden box. It has become a bit of an expectation now, that I'll read to her. I am not sure how I feel about it. I've left great-granny Irene's letters at home, so I start reading from my grandmother Annie's journal instead.

ANNIE, 1950

Mother and Granny Marie told me they made certain I kept my job in service at the big house by telling the lady they knew who had fathered Harriet's bairn. Granny Marie guessed it was one of the lady's sons. We'd all grown up together, playing in the grounds. Clearly, Harriet played a little more than I did. Mum had chortled, telling me about the lady going white, grey, and then back to white again at the news.

'But how did you know?' the lady had apparently asked.

'Those downstairs always know about those upstairs,' was my grandmother's answer.

'The bairn will be taken care of, but no one can know,' the lady had insisted.

But in our small village, everyone knew. Although they would all deny it in public, everyone knew those at the big house gave Harriet money to keep quiet.

Mother told me she said to the lady at the time, 'I'll leave you to think about that,' as her parting shot. She had then turned her back on the lady and swanned away.

Later that day, Famie fell down the stairs, and all hell broke loose. The lady said no more about me leaving. The police came, but everyone explained what a clumsy lassie Famie was, and those stairs were never built for running down.

We'd all tripped on the kitchen steps plenty of times before, carrying too much. They were so much narrower than the steps upstairs—an accident waiting to happen.

HARRIET CALLED HER BAIRN AGNES, *and she took her surname—Moleman. That name was to be mine, too, as Harriet's brother proposed to me before the war. I had known Alec all my life. Mother was furious.*

She got on fine with James and Helen, his parents, but hated William, the grandfather. Granny Marie couldn't stand the mention of his name either, although she never told me why. Granny Marie didn't speak to me for a while after I told her. She left me with the words,

'Nae good will come of that family, let me tell you. Any relation of William Moleman isn't good enough for my grandchild.'

My brother John taught dancing in the town, in the ice-cream parlour. A miracle occurred when he was a child. No one thought he would live when he was born. His legs were all twisted, his breathing poor. The doctor had written out his death certificate in preparation and told mother he wouldn't last the night.

My mother, Irene, sat up all night and rubbed whisky on his lips to revive him, and he lived on. He could speak well enough, and although his walk was quaint, he danced like Fred Astaire.

He charged for dancing lessons, and I helped him when I was younger, making sure he got on and off the bus safely and taking the money. I was barely sixteen, too young to be on the premises late at night. One of the boys from Prestonpans, Martin, asked me to dance. I didn't recognise him, but thought him handsome, so we danced. As we glided across the floor, I felt his strong arms take control. I felt like a film star. He frowned then, scrutinising my face.

'How old are you?'

'Sixteen.'

He stopped our dance and led me off the floor by my wrist, his back to me. My Hollywood moment was over.

'Sixteen! I'm twenty.' He took me back to my brother. 'She's too young to be here.' John shrugged.

'I'm here to help out,' I interrupted.

'You should not be here at this age,' he announced first to me, and then to John. 'You need to keep a better eye on your wee sister. She's just a lassie.' He shook his head and ambled away.

WHEN THE WAR BEGAN, Alec travelled away to fight. We suffered through rationing. We managed all right, with me working at the big house. They had stockpiles of food in tins, which did the duration. I'd nick the odd tin now and then.

Blackouts happened often. All the houses needed shutters to block out the light, and the streetlights were out. John mentioned bumping into lampposts and apologising to them because it was so dark.

Bombings occurred, but the village was safe enough, although I could watch the planes heading to Glasgow overhead. We owned an Anderson shelter, but many didn't bother going to the shelter, instead hiding under tables. My job was to put my younger sisters to bed with their siren suits on, so if the sirens woke them, they could head to the shelter straightaway, wearing Mickey Mouse gas masks. Those were long years, but they eventually came to an end.

Sadie's man returned from the war to two new, dark-skinned children who needed to be explained. She had to hold her hands up about the Italian from the prisoner of war camp. Her man simply said, 'Oh well, I've been away a while and not been innocent either.' And that was that.

Granddad Thomas died in 1945. He could not cope with another war and burying more of his children and family. Two of my uncles never made it back, and another went missing in action at Dunkirk.

Alec wrote sometimes, and I waited for him to return, but the letters came less and less. Once the war ended and he was due to return, our wedding was planned for two months after. I was working in the shop on day, when Freda sauntered in.

'I've just seen Alec,' she announced with a cocky smirk.

'You can't have. He's not due back yet.'

'I spoke to him.'

'Where?'

'He was at the bus stop, heading to Dalkeith to go out with his friends.'

I threw the rolls about the shop and flung the bread on the shelf so hard I could not think. How had he come home early and not told me? After work, I ran home.

'He's got till 7 o'clock, and I'm going to the dancing,' I raged to mother, my hands on my hips.

'But the cards and invitations are all printed,' pleaded mother, in despair.

'I don't care,' I burrowed my thumbs into my back.

'But they're ready to go out,' she argued. She fetched Granny Marie.

Seven o'clock came and went, and I sat with my coat on. Granny Marie and mother watched on. I paced up and down until half past. My legs were dyed with tea, and I'd drawn a seam down the back of them, ready to go out.

I checked the mirror. My red hair was set prettily, and I sprayed on a touch of perfume—Soir de Paris.

Well, tonight, it had to be Soir de Prestonpans, as that was where the dancing took place, and the bus was leaving in 10 minutes.

My mother gazed at me with a perplexed expression, shook her head, and threw Granny Marie a begging look. Granny Marie shrugged and said, 'Let her be, Irene.'

I inhaled and strode to the door.

Granny Marie held mother back as she started to bar my way. 'What are we going to do?' asked mother.

'Let her go, Irene.'

Mother frowned.

'I'm away for the bus.' I announced, knowing I had missed it and I would have to walk the whole way. Never mind, I thought as I marched. A long walk always felt good to me.

Glancing back, I saw Granny Marie in the window with a smile on her face.

After the dance, I let Martin, the boy who had danced with me as a young girl, walk me home. As soon as I got back, I threw the wedding invitations in the fire.

FORTY-TWO

RHIANNON

ON MY WAY HOME, I find myself at the last opening by the park. *Why did I dare take this way from The Lagoons towards the bridge? Then again, why shouldn't I? I'm heading home, with a bit of a diversion.*

Suddenly, Kim is on the left side of the road, heading towards me. Right on cue, she wanders into the opening from the main road into the cul-de-sac.

I slow right down, holding back. Her house must be one of the houses on the left. I sit on the bench side on, so I can watch where she goes. There are six blocks, two on the left, two in the middle, and two on the right. Each block has two semi-detached houses.

I watch her walk past the first block on the left to the second block on the left. She opens a gate and enters. I can't make out which one, but I am down to two houses now. *Maybe the far away one.*

I sit on the bench facing away from their cul-de-sac, overlooking the river. The river meanders away to the left, to the start of the beach. A huge piece of driftwood lies on the far bank, recently swept downstream by the heavy rains or swept back up from the sea with the tide. It resembles a dragon—if a dragon possessed a snake's undulating body with wings sticking upwards and downwards into the sand. Dragon number two lives behind me, with her snake. *Robbie the jobbie,* I snigger.

I slide my hand into my pocket, feeling the bulk of my grandmother Annie's letters, which I took from the box at the care home. Given Mum's newfound media celebrity, I figure the letters are better off with me—besides, they're finally getting interesting.

FORTY-THREE

ANNIE, 1963

Dear Nettie,

Mum said you wanted to hear more stories from the village and all about our lives there. I'm not that good at remembering everything or even writing I think, but I always kept a diary, as you know.

Mind you when I got to thinking about everything, it all came back as clear as I was there. You'll know pretty much everything about us growing up together. There's not much sisters who share a room don't know about each other, so I'll start with after I got married.

In 1950, Alec moved to the prefabs, across the road from where Martin and I moved once we married in 1947.
For years, Alec remained unmarried. He kept to himself, dodging up and down to the newly built bowling club every day for a drink. By the end of the fifties, the village had grown from just a row of houses to

having a church, a garage, a co-operative shop, and the Institute—for dancing on a Saturday night.

Alec considered himself important and he gained a position on the committee for the Institute. One of our cousins sang in there, and he didn't pay her. You'll maybe remember which one?

I remember Granny Marie, who lived with Mum by then, saying, 'Come out from among them. Wipe the dust from your feet, as they are nothing but a bunch of whoores and whooremaisters.' It became a saying of hers, whenever anyone slighted our family, and she'd always announce it with venom. You'll know this well, Nettie! I've heard you say it yourself.

She never had any time for Alec. Granny Marie and my mother both mentioned they wouldn't shed a single tear when William, his father, died either.

The gala took place every year, with an elected king or queen. I always imagined my grandmother, Marie, as the queen bee.

She told me the Queen and Princess Margaret had attended the gala in the 1930s, when they'd visited the big house up the road in Carberry. She told me with a cackle that as soon as she saw the cars coming with the royal flags, she turned her back. She waited until they were nearly on her, and then spun to face the field. She could not cope with anyone having more power than her, and she'd curtsy to no one.

My daughter could never win the races and competitions at the gala, because Alec judged them. He stood there, wearing a large rosette, as she ran up to claim her prize, and then he gave it to the girl who'd come in second. She never understood why she didn't win. But he hated me, since I'd rejected him after the war.

My man, Martin, worked hard. Granny Marie bossed everyone, insisting we hand over our wages to her to be distributed as she saw fit. She saved it up for our annual trip to Blackpool. We loved it there, taking in the sea air.

Martin wasn't happy about giving her all his money, so when he did overtime, he crept his motorbike past her house so as not to wake her. That way, she wouldn't realise he had extra pounds coming in. He hid that money in the cistern of our toilet, unbeknownst to me. I wished he had told me, as I needed a plumber to fix the toilet when it wasn't working. Of course, Granny Marie arranged it, as we had no way of paying the plumber otherwise. She had all the cash, and with it all the power. When the plumber approached Granny Marie for payment, he mentioned he found a bag of money in there. She marched down and confiscated the lot.

In 1958, when Alec was thirty-seven, he returned from a visit to his family in Carluke with a bride of nineteen. I heard rumours Maureen was his cousin. Granny Marie claimed her fireplace was a disgrace, and she wasn't quite all there.

Soon, her sister, Vera, arrived, and moved into their home too. There were rumours of a strange set-up. The sister drank in the club with men and got a name for herself. She had two children, and no one knew the fathers, so folk made up their own stories. The lot of them were wild.

Due to Martin being a miner, we got free coal which we kept in the coal bunker outside. Soon enough, I noticed the levels going down too quickly. I felt certain someone was stealing it. I made a mark on all the top pieces: a cross.

The following day, after the top layer of coal had been skimmed off, I made my way to the house across the road.

Maureen threw herself in front of me to stop me going in their bunker.

'You can't say we stole your coal. What are you looking for anyway? Every bit of coal looks the same. You can't say it's yours.'

I pushed her aside. 'No? Mine is marked with a cross.'

She froze.

I picked up two pieces and showed her the markings. No police were involved, but she didn't do it again. The fact everyone knew about it was punishment enough for life. Life means life in small villages.

I banged on Maureen's door another time, about Vera's tykes, but instead of listening she dragged me in. Maureen and her sister threw me about the hallway and flung me out onto the street. 'Dinnae come to our door again,' they yelled. There was something every week with them.

The worst event happened when I caught that floozie Vera with Martin in the close. I'd seen it all. She started it, falling about with the drink and lifting her skirt. Martin had stood to watch the show, and I gave him hell for that. But when she pushed herself against him, he wriggled away. I told Granny Marie all about it. When she insisted it could be dealt with, I felt better.

Hope that is all right for you, Nettie. You'll have plenty stories of your own. I mind you gave Maureen a good slapping in the close, too. What was that about again?

Anyway, hope you are all well.

All my love,

Annie

FORTY-FOUR

RHIANNON

'MAD TRACE!' Jan announces, as she plonks herself onto the chair.

"What about her?' I glance behind me to check she isn't there.

'Mad Trace is back in prison!' she exclaims with joy. 'I mean, you've got to wonder. Angela and her both in the clink, and they were at school together too. Some class that must have been.' Jan sniggered.

'What for now?' I ask.

'Stabbed her man.'

'The new one? That old guy? Is he okay?'

'Yeah.'

'So she never actually killed anyone?'

'Not for want of trying.'

'Aye, she just wasn't very good at it.'

We laugh.

'Been so much tragedy in this area. Darren dying, too.' I wantto bring up the toilet conversation, and how I'm sure Kim is a killer. I want to remind Jan that Kim had told her the plan. I blanch, swallow, and open my mouth to blurt it all out, but Jan interrupts my thoughts.

'I saw Kim.'

'Right.' *That name!* I think. *Was she reading my thoughts?*

'Yeah, well ... she's in my hockey club.'

'You play hockey?'

'No! To hell with that. The bairns go, not me. I asked Kim to join us, but you see, she's always busy.'

I sigh with relief after checking Kim isn't behind me either and noting to remember to sit facing the café door next time. *I understand what Kim is like. Does Jan?*

Jan, deep in thought, pauses longer than usual. 'She's not a bad person.'

I never claimed she was. Does Jan have doubts?

'But there was the hockey club money,' Jan goes on. 'She didn't need to steal it, so technically she hasn't.'

'What's this? What money?'

'Some folks are saying she stole the money from the hockey club. We had the fundraiser, and she said she would deposit the money, but it's not in yet. I said she probably forgot to put it in, but she's going to, right?'

'Oh, right. Like she was meaning to do it.'

'Yes, exactly. It's been a year, but she's just not got round to it. And, to be fair, they've been hounding her about it. That would be annoying.'

I nod.

'It's not like she isn't going to. I don't know how much it was, about 300 pounds, but that's not much to Kim, see. She doesn't see what the fuss is over a wee bit of money 'cos her and Rob are so well off.'

How nice for her. I make a conscious effort to stop my eyes from rolling.

'I mean, have you seen their house? Everything in it is perfect. Her kitchen cost thousands. She's always got the best. And he's got the best car. She's always been like that. Kim always had everything just right, even when she was with Darren.' Jan pauses to gaze out the window. 'And then, of course, she got the life insurance and the house and the pub after that.' She half giggles, adding, 'She's not needing to steal a thousand pounds of charity money for God's sake.'

'I thought it was 300 quid?'

'Well, yeah, but she took the yearly dues as well, and the money from the car boot sale another time. She's a bit flaky, a bit wrapped up in herself, but it will be on the to-do list. She's not greedy, not one bit. We went shopping one time and she bought me a bag. Seven hundred pounds it cost. She's generous ... see?' She holds up the bag.

'Aye, I see.'

'I said I liked it. That's all it took. She is so kind in that way.' Jan strokes the bag, but she doesn't seem convinced by her own words.

Yesterday, I was brave enough to lean on a tree by the bench and watch Kim and her husband leave in a red car. I'm terrible at recognising cars. What kind of car is it? An estate?

I'd find out. The registration ends OBV. Obviously. I'll remember that.

I'd volunteered to deliver leaflets to fundraise for the am dram. I sauntered around, stuffing them into letterboxes. Hers was number 3 or 4. I searched for clues. Jan's description of perfection fitted number 4, as the pots were neat. I peered around the side. I spotted a tree through the gate railing on the right-hand side and was positive this was the house. The next house had an unkempt garden with a summer seat peeling with paint. The sign on number 4 read, Beware of the dog.

A dog barked at the window, and the curtain flapped as he threw himself against the glass. Yorkshire terriers are not terrifying under normal circumstances, but I jumped out of my skin.

I snorted. The next-door neighbour came out. She

stared right at me, curbing my giggles. I handed her a leaflet, which she took and put it in her letterbox, which was strange. Then it dawned on me: She's not a neighbour. She wore an NHS uniform and lit a cigarette as soon as she was beyond the doorstep.

'Ah, you working here?' I thought out loud.

'Aye,' she snapped. Clearly surprised anyone was interested in her at all, her angry face melted and she opened up. 'Yeah, I'm a carer.'

She seemed suddenly glad of the interaction. 'She used to get out a lot, but not so good on her legs now. She can about manage the toilet along the corridor, but she is ninety-two. Her daughter comes on a Saturday once a week, but she has her own family and works too.'

'How does she manage the stairs?'

'They have a bedroom downstairs. They only use the bottom part these days,' she explained.

I realised that the elderly lady would not be able to see the neighbour's garden from her place, so I'd avoid Saturdays if I ever came again. So much for confidentiality.

As she spoke, her eyes were cast downwards. I gazed over to the block in the middle of the cul-de-sac. It was at a right angle to number 4, with no windows overlooking their back garden at all. I was excited by all I had learnt. I didn't know what I was doing, but it felt wrong, which was thrilling.

On a lamppost near the entrance to the cul-de-sac someone had tied a black-and-white checked printed scarf.

Is it hers? I watched it flutter in the wind. Do I take it? What do I do with it?

I chose to steal it. A souvenir. At the back of the houses, instead of taking The Lagoons path, I found another route to the racecourse along the back. I have been getting up a lot of steps, getting fitter, noticing I can bend easier, walk further without tiring. I used the tree I had observed from the front of the houses as a landmark.

I'd taken a knife with me. You can't carry a knife legally; it is an offensive weapon. But I'd bought the Swiss army knife from the shop in the high street after meeting Jan. A lovely red one.

I've always admired them: the feel fitting my hand, taking all the bits out and putting them back. I was never allowed one as a child. Now that I'm old enough, I bought one easily.

What do I need it for? It's useful.

That's what I'd say if anyone asked.

I'm just walking, after all—that's all I'm doing.

FORTY-FIVE

RHIANNON

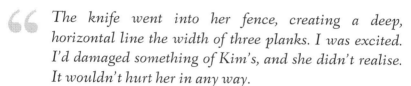The knife went into her fence, creating a deep, horizontal line the width of three planks. I was excited. I'd damaged something of Kim's, and she didn't realise. It wouldn't hurt her in any way.

No one else saw it. Did it really happen?

I felt happier than I had when I was talking to the carer woman. When you shy away from people, it's not from them; it's from the way they make you feel.

The one thing that might help my loneliness—time spent around people—throws me into a fit of fear. I understand that other people are perhaps the main component of a contented life, so I do not understand the swift stab of panic I experience at their presence. I blame myself. There must be something wrong with me.

My flat seems empty and quiet now, after the barrage of noise and hilarity from Jan and my adventure today. I wonder if Jan is sitting quietly at home with Terry.

Even watching TV is difficult alone. It's a chore

with no one to turn to and say, 'Who's that? What was he in? Oh, that one with that guy.'

Time and events vanish when no one comments. There is no one to notice that I'm not crying. I've just something in my eye at the sad bits. No one can hear my hollow laughter at a comedy—apart from the neighbours. They know I live alone. They'll think I've gone mad.

I feel mad.

I also feel compelled to write all this down. If I don't write it down, it's as if it never happened. I'd been back here just months, and it already seems as if ten years have been deleted in a snap of my fingers, like they never happened.

Magicians make things disappear and people are amazed. But when people disappear? My grandmother's journals suggest life is a disappearing trick, and that magic happens far more than you think.

FORTY-SIX

Dear Nettie,

Here's another instalment. I've had time to think about all we did. Remember we always used to go to Blackpool? Well, this is the trip you missed, as you were on the lie down and due that very weekend.

Granny Marie hired a man with a bus to drive us there. The whole village came, including Alec's tribe. On the way there, I sat by Agnes Moleman, who Granny Marie tolerated, despite hating most of her family.
'Hi, Senga!' I said, as I threw myself into my seat.
Agnes rolled her eyes. 'Don't call me that. It's Agnes.'
'Oh, all right.'

Agnes considered herself better. Her mother Harriet, on her own, could afford so much more than anyone else. She sent Agnes to a private school run by the Red Cross and owned by the biscuit people. She only returned home at holiday time.

Agnes told me she hated it, as she had to rise at 6 am for chores. It was a strict school. The children got just one pound per term as allowance for shoe repairs or thread.
Everyone wondered how Harriet had afforded it, but I understood. Agnes made out that she got in on a scholarship, but she didn't. We both know who her dad was, Nettie! She was clever enough, though. She trained to become a teacher.

Agnes's fiancé was on the bus too. I forget his name. He seemed well off, smartly dressed and from Edinburgh. We didn't speak to him. We didn't get the chance.

On our first day, one of the bairns made a dash across the road to the sand, not looking. Agnes' fiancé jumped up and ran after him, pushing him out of the way of an oncoming tram, only for it to hit him square on.

Her fella looked just like he was sleeping, as he lay on the ground. We couldn't wake him. Agnes was screaming at the bairn, shaking him. 'What did you do that for, you stupid, stupid child?'

Mother grabbed her as she fell to her knees. All of our crowd were focused on Agnes's man and the tragedy on the seafront. No one noticed me sneak away after Vera. She'd been drinking a lot, as usual, all day. That night, she slipped off the pier in the dark into the sea.

I thought you'd like that one, Nettie. I remember you gave Maureen and Vera a doing in the street one time. Took them both on and won. I'll never forget it.

Mind on, and keep these letters to yourself, hen!

Give my regards to the family.

All my love,
Annie

FORTY-SEVEN

ROB

Dear Diary,

We enjoyed episodes of calm, but then, out of the blue, obstacles sprang up to surprise us, drama dredged up from nowhere. Small slices of unnerving stress left me feeling bad, guilty, and, in the end, persecuted.

We strolled to the train hand-in-hand. I hoped we could always live like this, contented and chilled. I had no indication anything was about to happen, no sense of impending doom.

Our seats were not together. Late to book, we couldn't reserve all four seats together. Our plan was to meet up on the train with another couple due to embark at York. Kim had arranged it all.

I didn't get mad that she'd left it to the last minute. Of course, the seating issue could have been avoided if she'd let me sort it. I would have arranged it all months in advance. I didn't say anything. Well, it had already been done, and, of course, it would blow up into an argument, so it wasn't worth it. We'd all arrive in London eventually and would enjoy a lovely holiday.

On the train, we had three seats together and a single separate. Kim graciously told me she would sit in the single seat. The single seat was by the door, and the three seats at a table were booked at the far end. She said, as they were my friends, I could sit there with them and enjoy a catch-up.

I sat alone until a lady my age, wearing a red cardigan, entered the carriage and sat in the fourth seat. I ruminated over suggesting a swap with Kim, but for some reason, I felt glad to have a break from her. Also, Kim had suggested she sit in the single seat, so I didn't want to upset her by changing plans again. She'd say I was telling her what to do and didn't appreciate all the trouble she had gone to arranging it all. I decided to leave things as they were.
I nodded a hello to red-cardigan lady, who said, 'I wonder if anyone is going to sit in the other seats,' as she peered at the signs above the aisle. 'My friends are getting on at York,' I said.
She seemed disappointed.

I toyed with the idea that maybe she fancied me, but I came to the conclusion she wanted a seat for her bag, which she plonked down next to her for the first half of the trip. I shifted my feet to allow the bag extra legroom, such was my impossible politeness. After exchanges about the weather, our small talk slipped into silence.

By Newcastle, I had to visit the loo and stretch my legs. I headed down to the front of the carriage, instead of going to the nearest toilet at our end. I planned to speak to Kim for a minute, in her single seat by the aisle. Her head nodded as she was in deep conversation with the bald man next to her. I stood in the queue for the loo next to them, and she did not even notice me. I coughed. She didn't turn. I started to fidget and shift from foot to foot. She carried on conversing.

'Ahem. Hiya!' I said with a smile, sending my foot over to touch her shoe in a small kick. A blonde woman in the adjacent double seat glanced up at me, and then at Kim, to watch her reaction. There was none. Noticing Kim fail to even acknowledge me, the blonde screwed up her face, all the while pretending to read her book. Kim swivelled her head and glanced up at me. The bald man, noticing her attention was elsewhere, followed her gaze. Still she did not respond. Her expression was blank. She returned to her conversation with the bald man. Baldy stared at me for a moment, shook his head, shrugged, and carried on talking. The blonde woman opposite tutted and whispered to the woman near her. She gave me a hard stare. I froze for a minute, reddened, and then entered the toilet, which was now free.

I peered in the mirror at my warm, red face and asked myself, 'What was that? What happened? Why is there always something different? Why is there always a surprise?

There was always a side-sweeping tackle from behind that I didn't see coming. It tossed me up in the air, so I could not even make sense of what part of the world I was in and what space I took up. I chastised myself. I felt daft for reacting to her weird behaviour. How could a man be scared to interrupt his own wife when talking to a total stranger? Had I been rude? It's difficult to decide when to interrupt sometimes. I hated it when people left me hanging. She seemed offended I'd had the nerve to give her a playful nudge, but I didn't kick, I tapped. Why was she ignoring me?

I decided to speak to her when I got out of the toilet. I exited and stood in front of them both, in the aisle. They carried on talking, heads together. I felt myself getting agitated.
The blonde woman stood, and I moved to let her out, but as she passed, she whispered, 'What are you doing?'
'I'm just wanting to speak to...'
'I'd go sit down, if I were you. Stop bothering that couple.'

Red again, I rushed back to my seat.

'Are you okay?' queried red-cardigan woman.

'Yes. Fine,' I replied curtly.

The ticket collector approached minutes later.

'Hi, can I have a word? The lady down there tells me you have been behaving strangely?'

'My wife is down there.'

'Your wife?'

'Yes, the lady there at the front with ...' I indicated Kim.

'Yeah, about that. The woman says you kicked that lady, yeah?' He smiled, but the inquisition was deliberate.

'Well, yes.' I smiled back.

Red-cardigan woman, who was listening, raised her eyebrows.

'Well ... not kicked,' I explained, 'just a friendly wee knock for attention, like this.' I acted out the movement towards the shoe of the red-cardigan woman. She pulled her foot away, eyes wide, and threw a glance at the older couple across the aisle, who had become attentive to the developing situation.

'Yeah, right,' replied the ticket collector. He seemed unsure what to do. He paused, and then said, 'So, can I suggest that if you need you go to the toilet, you use the one nearest.' He indicted the toilet sign at this end of the carriage.

'But that's my wife down there.'

'Yeah. If you could do that.'

'I've not done anything. I just wanted to speak to my wife.'

'Okay.' The ticket collector appeared tired of all this. 'Look, I'm going to have to ask you to please stay in your seat.'

I settled down as instructed, used to getting told what to do. Orders I understood. My phone was out of charge, so I couldn't even text her, but based on her behaviour earlier, she might not even respond.

The train stopped at Durham, and I spotted the collector speaking to a colleague on the platform.
'Bit of a mix up.' I tried to speak to red-cardigan lady.
She pulled her paper up, put her earphones in, and crossed her legs.
Her body was knotted like my stomach.
The carriage whispered. 'He kicked some woman.'
'Probably a wife beater.'
'Maybe had a falling out.'
'Kicked a random stranger.'
'Bloody nutter,' huffed a large, older man across the way, louder than most.
'Shush, Frank!' scolded his wife, although the young student in front of him nodded her head in agreement.

I felt claustrophobic. To no one in particular, I announced, 'Wait until York. My friends Ishbel and Ian will get on, and they'll sort this out. And she is my wife. She can fix this.'
But she didn't. They no doubt judged that Kim wasn't my wife at all, but they didn't realise the games she could play.

When the train rolled into York station, I peered out of the window in anticipation. At the start of the platform, I couldn't spot them. They'll come into view at any minute, I thought, scanning the platform. The platform drained of people as those who wanted off dispersed and those who wanted on filtered in. I stared at the carriage doors, hoping for their arrival. When the train took off again, I concluded they must have got on at the far end and be making their way up the train. 'My friends will be here in a minute,' I declared out loud.

Red-cardigan woman pulled her cardigan over to cover herself up. I huffed. I was not looking at her like that.
Ten minutes passed.
'Where's your pals, then?' snorted big Frank. The student laughed, and Frank's wife couldn't help but join in.

I felt the rage grow in my face. 'Stuff this!' I jumped up. 'I'm going down to speak to her.'
Frank stood up and barred the way. 'No, you don't.'
I slumped back in my seat, to mutters of, 'Quite right' and 'I thought it was all going to kick off there.'

At Peterborough, an official appeared with the ticket collector behind him. 'I don't want to have to put you off the train,' he said, warning me to stay in my seat.
'I'm going to London with my wife.'
Red-cardigan woman sighed, shaking her head.
'She is down at the end—' I got cut off with a gesture that said Hold on, I'll check.

The official talked to Kim, who glanced back for a second but shook her head. Frank watched with intense concentration and whispered to his wife, 'See, told you!'
The guard sauntered up the carriage. 'Sir, you can stay on the train.'
'You are kidding!' interjected Frank.
'Francis!' scolded his wife again.
'But please don't move. No more until London. We are late as it is.'

The train moved on and I sat in silence, sometimes catching the disapproving eye of the passengers who had judged me already. I picked up the dead phone and stared at my bag on the shelf, where my charger lay in the zipped pocket. I stood up to retrieve it.
'Sit down, mate,' a voice filtered in from behind and others chipped in.
'Leave it. Keep out of it.'
'He just needs to sit down.'
'Dunno what your problem is, pal. We all want to get to London with no bother,' said Frank.
I sat down again, resigned that London was close.

Once there, Frank made sure I got off at our end of the carriage. I

disembarked to see Kim on the platform, still chatting to the bald man.
He embraced her, kissed her on the cheek, and then strolled away. She
waited for me.
'Kim.'
'Hi.' She smiled that full grin of hers.
'What happened?' I asked.
'How do you mean? I met a nice man and had a right fun chat.'
'You ignored me!'
'What? When?' She frowned
'On the train. I went to the loo and spoke to you.'
'I never saw you.'
'I nudged your foot.'
'Nope. Didn't notice.'
I knew she had.
'But the guard spoke to you.'
'Yeah, that was weird.' There was a pause in the conversation. It
became clear she was not going to expand on that subject.
'You wouldn't believe the carry-on I had.'
She cut me off with an exasperated sigh. 'Oh, you! Always a drama.
Let's find a taxi.'

I understood not to say any more. What had she said to the guard? Had
she denied being my wife? Had she claimed I was abusing her? I
would never know. She didn't want to talk about it. It was best not to
pursue any further questioning.

'Where are Ian and Ishbel? They never came on?'
'They texted me that they got the earlier train. They're at the hotel
now.'
'When? When did they text?'
'Earlier.'
'When, though?'
'Just before we got on the train. Did you not get a text? I did.'
'My phone was out of charge.'

'Silly, there's power points on the train.'

'I know. I forgot, but then I couldn't get my charger. You never said they weren't coming when we got on the train.'

'I'm telling you now.' She gave me a hard stare, her grin fading in annoyance.

I spotted red-cardigan woman transfixed on us, removing her earphones with a look of confusion as Kim and I left together. I wanted to say something to Kim, but I saw disappointment on her face and was worried she might start something and spoil the fun. I was ready for her words of hate: The 'you are this, you are that' accusations. The echoes of previous arguments rang in my head above the hustle and noise of King's Cross. All those questions I asked gifted her something to mock, injected the adrenaline shot.

I strode by her side in silence in the dirty London air, feeling in the wrong but sensing deep, deep down that I was right somehow. The rest of me believed I shouldn't speak, indeed had learnt not to.

Why would she treat me this way if she loved me?
I felt a pill-sized righteousness buried in my core.

FORTY-EIGHT

RHIANNON

My heart is pumping. I know something she does not. I have one up on her. I finished the job today and just marched home. It's been the best exercise I've had in years. I am still ruminating on my handiwork.

No one goes along by the fences; there is no actual path there, just rough grass. To others, it might appear as if I'm taking a shortcut, I guess, or repairing something. First, I wandered along the park path between the houses and the beginning of the lagoon. That route always pleases me. It makes it feel like I have something to aim for, a purpose, rather than an aimless saunter. It always feels like an adventure.

I made my way to her back fence, far away from the park equipment and path. Anything different won't be seen from the main thoroughfares. Even in the open area, outwith the usual times, people were rarely there apart from lunch-time walkers or children after school. Today, it was empty apart from four kids playing with remote control cars a good bit away, making loud noises as they crashed into each other, enjoying the destruction of their precious property. There is a joy in deconstruction and damage, I suppose, which gives vandals a thrill. Destruction can feel as creative as building something.

Over the past few months, since I made the initial cut, I have chipped away at Kim's fence almost every day. Three whole planks I've cut completely across. I dropped into the hardware store and bought some fake ivy, some hinges, and a screwdriver. I took out the hinges and repaired each plank over time, covering the joins with the ivy. Every day I returned, cutting at the bottom of the planks. After several days, they hung free. Each plank can now move up and down.

Now that the three planks can hinge open, I have a hatch opening into Kim's garden. From the inside, they won't see anything because all the damage lies behind their shed. Between their garden shed and the fence is just a foot and a half of nothing except some grass that's reseeded. I enjoy the fact that Kim owns a scruffy area.

Of course, I worry that I might never fit through the hatch. It's eighteen inches wide, but with all this walking, I've lost more weight. I'm so busy thinking these days, I forget to eat.

I take pleasure in this journaling, and in reading the others too. But I can't write more now, I'm cold from my march, and too excited, so I plan to shower and use all my expensive toiletries. Sometimes, time goes by and then I realise I am thirsty or hungry or it's dark. But lately, I've become obsessed with identifying, pre-empting, and meeting my own needs. I'm like a boxer getting ready for a fight. I'm in training for the match, the big show. I pause a dozen times an hour to take my own pulse of desire.

Do I need water? Tea? Coffee? A snack? A nap? Different music? A break?

Identifying a necessity creates urgency, something to do. I have someone to care for: me. I will shower, and then I will moisturise my skin, although no one will feel it on them. Then I will put on clean pyjamas and put fresh sheets on the bed. I will sleep well tonight.

FORTY-NINE

RHIANNON

I CATCH Kim's husband going to reception as I enter the care home. I stare at him, eyes wide and mouth open. No wonder he is staring too.

Was that a nod hello?

'Bertie's mum is here,' Mum says when I enter her room.

'Who is Bertie?'

'His mum owned the farm, you remember? He worked in the shop with you. There he is over there.'

I stare across the hall in the direction of her nod to spy Kim's dimple-chin himself sitting with his mum.

It *is* Bertie—*the boy from the village*. I had connected the man Kim had leant against from the pub, and the chap washing her car—Rob—but I'd forgotten I'd met him before that.

I knew him as a boy.

I stand up to peer at him and creep towards the door. When he glances up, I quickly close the door.

'What did you do that for?' Mum asks.

I ask myself the same question. *Because I couldn't cope with him being the boy.*

I plan to speak to Lesley about getting Mum moved out of Agnes Moleman's death room, but when I return to the reception area, Rob is waiting to speak to her too.

'Hi,' I begin, armed with the knowledge of who he actually is.

'Hello.'

'I used to live in the village. We worked at the shop together.'

'Oh, God yes! Em ... Rhona?'

'Rhiannon,' I correct him. I am forgotten.

'Oh sorry, Rhiannon. Yes, of course. God, you were just a wee lassie.'

'Yeah! You were a slightly bigger boy.'

'I'm a lot bigger now.' He pats his belly, and I giggle.

'Bertie, right?'

'Yeah. Well, Rob, these days.'

Our conversation stalls.

'Yeah. Mum's here,' we both say at once.

'Ah,' we say in unison.

'Look me up,' Rob says, as Lesley indicates she will speak to him now.

Oh, I will, and I already have.

I think I'm smart again, and then I remember he was the boy with the card, and my heart sinks.

AFTER VISITING MOTHER, I amble around the village, expecting to meet familiar faces but spotting none. There are more and more new people every week, all incomers—I snort at that. I have been gone years, but I'm still a local. Although the social club has gone, the shop is still there. It has changed, although the doors and fittings and the main staircase remain. One handle is worn down, but the other is not. It was always on the side no one opened. It was locked most of the time. I used the tarnished right-hand door handle to enter and glanced around at the more modern arrangements. The shell appears unchanged. It makes me reflect on my childhood in the village. If someone had asked me about my first job, I'd have told them about the pub, but it wasn't the pub, was it? Could I really count the corner shop? My Aunt Nettie had worked in the shop and used to take me there at the weekends, to give my mother some peace no doubt.

I was only nine years old—people would call it child labour now —but they gave me a wee pay packet with some coins in it at the end of the week. I stacked things on shelves, counted the money, tidied things up. I was a quiet child, never a nuisance, although Kimberly believed so. Kim worked there as the Saturday girl at nearly fifteen years old.

'What are you bringing her for?' she'd ask Auntie.

'She's fine.'

'She's a pain.'

Then the boy joined us. He was a beautiful boy with brown hair, a wonderful smile and kind eyes. He lit up the room whenever he entered it, although my mum said he was too forward. I adored him. He spoke to all the old ladies and to me, telling terrible jokes.

One Valentine's Day, he gave me a card. It had no question mark or guess who; instead, it was signed boldly by the sweet thirteen-year-old boy. My heart swells thinking about it. He had probably given a card to everyone in the shop; he was that kind of boy.

Then Kimberly found out. When I proudly showed her the card, she snatched it off me.

'You made that up, you wee liar.' She tore it up and threw it in a puddle. 'Did you steal that card off the shelf and write it yourself?'

'No.' I grabbed the pieces from the mud.

'Why are you going red then?'

'I'm not.' My lip shook, and I bit down to stop it.

'Stop embarrassing yourself.'

Bertie appeared at the door.

'Did you give her a card?

'No,' he whimpered, fear in his eyes.

I ran out and cried all the way home—not for the boy, not for her, not for anything but for my humiliation. *What if she told everyone I made it up, and he backed her up?*

Auntie Nettie only took me to the shop one more time, but he wasn't there. Kimberly was. When we finished for the day, we couldn't find her to lock up. Auntie Nettie was huffing, puffing and swearing, searching for her.

I spotted Kim with a cigarette in hand at the side of the building. She was facing the wall, with Bertie so close it seemed as if she had him pinned. I stopped.

'Get away from up there, you pair!' Auntie shouted.

Kimberly turned around and laughed right at me. The boy appeared upset.

I blocked the card incident from my mind for years.

The boy moved away to England.

How could I forget the boy Kimberly stole from me as a child? The same boy she intercepted at the pub on my leaving do. The same man who now lives happily ever after with perfect Kim in her fancy perfect house.

FIFTY

ROB

Dear Diary,

Four years in, Kim suffered a miscarriage. It became clear we would have no children. We were both devastated, and it took our relationship in another direction. It didn't make us closer, as shared grief might.

She started going out a lot, leaving me at home and coming in very late. She refused my offers to pick her up as her taxi service, snipping, 'You checking on me?'

She argued more and became aggressive again. After a few months, I became suspicious she was cheating on me. My insecurity and fear of deception crippled any hope of a settled life.

At least things seemed calm on the violence front, until Kim claimed to have heard a rumour I had been sleeping with someone else. She refused to tell me who had informed her of this lie. She used some texts

I'd sent her as proof. She maintained they had been sent to her by mistake and were meant for another woman, her friend Sheona.

A few weeks after the cheating accusations, Kim invited her friends over, including Sheona. Everything was well at the beginning. Everyone was enjoying themselves. I acted as drinks host, and perhaps the drinks flowed too well. I didn't see the harm, as long as conviviality resulted. Then, out of nowhere, Kim announced, 'I know the truth.' Her face twisted with rage as she switched to hateful mode.
'I'm sorry. What do you mean?' asked one of the girls.
'You and Sheona,' she announced, giving me a venomous stare.

Her friends appeared horrified. 'Kim, are you okay?'
'Here, you've had a couple of drinks too many.'
One friend put her arm around her and sat her down. They had probably seen her bitchy before, but not in full-on evil form.
'You see him flirting with her right in front of me? You see him?' She sobbed.
'I've not noticed ... ' one friend started, glancing at me.
She turned on Sheona. 'And don't say anything about not knowing anything about this, lady! I've seen the texts.'
The girls all stared at Sheona.
'I've not got any texts,' she insisted, flustered, and got her phone out.
'Deleted no doubt!' snapped Kim.
Sheona put the phone away. 'Honestly, nothing is going on.'
Kim kept shouting as Sheona and I refuted her claims, but she wouldn't listen. I decided to extract myself from the situation.

After thirty minutes, I made my way back to the house. All of her friends had all gone. Kim stood on the doorstep waiting for me. 'You have been harassing Sheona.'
'No.'
'I've worked out it wasn't her anyway. It's all cleared up. The girls were great, but they know what you are now, how you are to me.'

'What have you said?'
'They know all about you and your cheating with that tramp, whoever she is!'

Then, out of the blue, she attacked. I managed to break free and stumbled into the bedroom, dodging the shoes and plates that followed me. I tried to push the bed up against the door, but Kim barged in after me. I pushed her onto the bed and managed to escape and sleep in the car. Little did I realise her claims were a cover, or a projection, of what she was doing herself.

FIFTY-ONE
RHIANNON

NOSY BY NATURE, social media is my guilty pleasure. I try Facebook, raiding first Kim's page, and then his.

His page is very closed, nothing to see except a profile picture of the car I had seen in their street. I can't see his friends list, which is set to private.

I scroll back to Kim's page. We share mutual friends—folk from the village and the town, people like Jan, who we used to work with. I have enough friends to add her without raising suspicion, but I pause before sending the friend request. Then, *bam*! It is done.

She accepts immediately. She must be as nosy as me.

I add everyone on her friends list with his surname, figuring they must be his relatives. Some accept; others do not. I want as many mutuals as possible.

I could add him later. First, I felt compelled to find out about the man who loves her and can live with her, and, if Jan is to be believed, about the devil who bullies her.

I drag the bins down the stairs, and by the time I climb back up, I have a Facebook request from the beautiful boy himself.

We already have a handful of friends in common, so it isn't

suspicious in the slightest. I look through all his photos with different eyes, discovering he was a member of the golf club, rotary club, and the pony club.

Christ, he sounds a right arse. He's Rob the knob for sure. Has she married her reflection? Is he the king to her queen?

Kim always said I was up myself. But this guy is on every football committee, every rugby committee and gala committee going, mingling and networking all he could.

I send him a message:

Thanks for the add. x

I cringe at the x but throw in just for luck. Maybe I can get away with saying it's my signature sign-off.

I notice that Kim was out with Sheona, her bitchy bestie, again last week, and snort, remembering another spat with her before I moved away a decade ago.

Back then, I thought I'd found my perfect job in Edinburgh. *This is the one,* I remember thinking, until I strode into the room for the interview and saw Sheona sitting on the panel. I dragged my way through the interview, half willing it to stop and mostly staring out the window behind the interviewers, rather than looking Sheona in the eye. Every time I blinked, I hoped it would turn out to be just a daydream. When bad things like that happened to me, I often felt as if I were watching a movie. I disassociated myself so I could plough on through.

I'd received a call about the outcome of the interview later in the week. There was no time to prepare before a call in those days, no caller ID. I thought I would just get a rejection letter, so the call felt like it came out of nowhere.

'Hi, it's Sheona McPherson.'

My whole body slumped, inside and out. *Listen to your gut,* people often say. My gut said, *'Oh no, not this!'*

'Just to let you know, you did not get the job.' For a morose woman with a naturally monotone voice, she sounded delighted.

'Yeah, that's fine. Thanks for letting me know.' I was ready with the goodbye.

'I have some feedback on your interview performance here.' I heard some flipping of paper, some shuffling.

'Okay.' I imagined her with the phone cradled under her chin as she flicked through her notes.

She took a single breath before trying to start with her list of criticisms. 'Can I go through that with you? Firstly...'

'Do you know what? No, thanks,' I replied.

She hesitated. 'Pardon.'

'No, thank you.'

'Surely you want to understand how you came across.'

'Not really.'

'Oh, well!' Sheona's joyful day ended.

'Bye-bye now,' I said chirpily, hanging up before she could even mutter cheerio.

FIFTY-TWO

ROB

Dear Diary,

The small things got me suspicious to begin with.

'Hi,' I said as she entered.
'Hello,' she said, taking off her coat and heading into the kitchen.
'You're late tonight.'
'Yeah. Working late'
'Okay. I thought there were appointments. Were people there until that time?'
'Meeting.' She half-sighed over the noise of the kettle boiling.
'You never mentioned there was a meeting on. That's never happened before?'
'Don't start!' She sat down with her tea.

The following day, I sat in a café waiting to meet her, but she didn't show up at all. She wouldn't answer her phone.
'I forgot, sorry,' she said later on. She apologised often, but I was not sure how many times she meant it.

'But ...'
'I said sorry!'
I never pursued it further.

*A week later, she told me, 'I'll be late tomorrow. I'm meeting Jan.
We're going to Legs, Bums and Tums.'*
'Okay. No problem.'

*True to her word, she didn't come home at the usual time. I stared at
my phone, thinking of texting her and asking her to bring something in
from the shops on her way home. That way, it might not appear as if I
was checking up on her. I'd have to hope she didn't perceive it that
way, even though she monitored my movements to the second. As I
stared at the phone, it lit up, causing me to fumble and drop it. It was
my friend Eddie. 'Hey, I'm in town for one night only—take or leave it.'
I paused. I was used to checking with Kim what I could do, but if she
wasn't there to ask permission, she might never find out. Surely, I
could go out. Eddie wasn't here often, and I'd known him for years.
'Where?'*
'The wine bar. The one at the corner.'
'Yes, why not? See you in half an hour.'

*Eddie was waiting outside the wine bar. We entered together, only to
catch Kim and three others—two men and another woman—sitting at
a table. The woman was not Jan, and this was not Legs, Bums and
Tums. Eddie approached her table to say hello, but I suggested we
leave them to their night out. Kim did not seem irritated in the
slightest.*

*When she left her table and strolled to the toilet, I got her alone.
'What are you doing? You told me you were going to Legs, Bums and
Tums.'*
'I was at Legs, Bums and Tums, and now I'm here.'

I recognised one of the men who worked with her at the accountants: Greg.

'Where's Jan? And why are these people here?'

'Jan left. We just bumped into one another.' She pushed past to sit with her friends.

I joined Eddie, who looked confused by the dynamic.

'You want to join them?' He gestured.

'No.'

'Okay, weird. But okay.'

'She would hate that.'

Later, she passed us at the bar when she left to head home.

'Greg will give me a lift,' she announced, breezing past. I didn't understand why, but I sensed I had betrayed her somehow and reckoned on repercussions back home. Eddie threw me a quizzical glance.

Thinking back to their interactions in social gatherings, Greg and Kim always acted too playful at times, too flirty, too familiar. 'How was the course?' I'd once asked her when her office staff had gone away for the weekend.

'Good. I was paired with Greg.'

'Gee, he's boring. Wouldn't want to be stuck in a lift with him,' I joked.

'How dare you speak about him like that? What a monster you are, sitting here judging people.'

Her reaction had not made sense, but I had imagined I was just being paranoid.

I checked her phone in my worst moments, until she started taking extreme care of it. I found nothing obvious. But reading cryptic back-and-forth messages still gave me an uneasy feeling. I craved proof—in *black and white—before confronting her. There was still much to lose: our marriage, our shared finances and assets. So I waited.*

I needed concrete evidence; otherwise, this could all exist in my imagination, and I already believed I was mad; she'd told me so enough times. I found myself acting strange, too, getting agitated. We took a break one day for someone's birthday at work, and Jan brought in a tray of cakes. As we hung around in a huddle, I overheard two of the guys joking about men getting henpecked by their wives. The more I listened, the redder I got. 'That's not funny guys,' I said.
They carried on. 'Did you hear about Sandra?' asked one.
'No.'
'Actual video CCTV footage of her up the alley with James from accounts.'
'Are you kidding?'
'I can send you it.'
'What a tart!'
'I know. She is a legend. I don't think there's man in here she hasn't been with.'
'Are you still seeing that married one?'
'Yeah, the married ones are the best'.
'How come?'
'You don't have to buy them dinner, in case they get caught, so they're cheaper dates, and they don't care.'
'About what?'
'They aren't looking for commitment. They've already got a ring on their finger, right?' The second guy laughed.
I lost my temper and tipped the jammie doughnuts right up in the air.

FIFTY-THREE

RHIANNON

AFTER SLEEPING POORLY, I decide on a stroll and some fresh air. I know where I'll end up. I can move where I want, when I want, but so can she. I keep thinking Kim is watching; in the past, she was always hovering around the corner. Often, I'd hear her coming. But sometimes, she appeared from nowhere. I'd end up talking in whispers at work, as she could take offence at the slightest thing. She would put me in my place, throwing in digs for nothing.

'Have you seen that programme?' she'd ask.

'No, I didn't like it.'

'You wouldn't. Do you watch *Corrie*?'

'No, I don't like soaps.'

'Typical!' she'd snip, and then not speak to me for the rest of the day, making me wish I'd said yes.

One time, I tried to watch her favourite show just so I could say something about it the next day, hoping she'd warm to me. She would say the most barbed things, which I was to brush off, but she jumped down my throat for insulting her favourite film. It felt a bit like how social media feels now. People attack you for liking the wrong things. The hive mind is affronted if you don't fancy the same film stars.

Everyone is angry all the time. Or maybe it is the stress of lockdowns. No one would say what people say on social media to someone's face —except Kim did for years.

As I stroll, I notice that people are vandalising things around town. I tut. *Why shit on your own doorstep?*

Mine isn't vandalism, I've decided. It's my constructive way of dealing with anxieties about my past. *Is it revenge? Yes, but it is productive.*

I've made a lovely hatch.

At the fence, one of the neighbours has lit a bonfire. I'm certain that's not allowed without permission, and Kim has washing out, so she'll have something to say about that.

On cue, I hear Kim in the garden, pulling the washing off the line and shouting over the fence. She goes quiet, and I lose track of her position. Then I hear her next door, arguing about the bonfire.

After checking no one is around, I try the hinge and then step onto her property. Behind the shed, I slip the hinge back down again behind me. I stand completely still, strangely satisfied to be the creepy weirdo I am. I'm the opposite of claustrophobic. I'm cosy and calm for a minute. Then I experience a loud banging against my rib cage.

My heart. Fear?

No, I'm excited.

Breathe! I remind myself.

I feel powerful.

THE SCENT of smoke from the bonfire draws a memory of the village back into my brain: Alec, coughing and shouting. I can't remember what. He was bent over, clutching a tea towel over his mouth. He ran at us, and then fell to his knees in the front garden.

Kim did not even react when he shouted at her. I can't remember what he said.

I give myself a shake. There is no time for reminiscing now. I need my wits about me.

Kim finishes arguing with the neighbour and disappears into her house, slamming the front door. I slip out through the hinged flaps.

I'm in charge now, Kim. I'm up to something. I'm plotting and planning, and you can't do anything about it. This queen has made her move, and you have no idea where I'll move next.

FIFTY-FOUR
ROB

Dear Diary,

Kim's favourite film was Brief Encounter. *I considered it sweet that she loved black-and-white films and could even quote from them. She'd often announce, 'It is awfully easy to lie when you know you are trusted implicitly.'*
I found it an unnerving quote. But she'd say, 'That's true, very true' and nod like a sage.

Had she been lied to before? Had that made her wary of trusting too much? Or was it just something she related to?

Others might consider it a warning: don't trust with all your heart, which just opens the door to lies. It's a huge advantage to a liar if they find someone who believes everything they say. If you aren't ever doubted, you're unlikely to be found out. If you are caught, it becomes the fault of the too-trusting party—for making it too easy. If Kim had stuck that quote that on the wall, it would have suited our home better than the 'Live, laugh, love' positive affirmation she'd stencilled on the dining room wall.

I wished I could stand up to Kim. But did I really? No, I wanted her to love me. I wanted to care about her without fear of upsetting her over nothing. But nothing I did measured up. I decided to improve myself; surely then I'd be easier to love.

She had wanted me once, when we were young, and then again when I returned from England to accept the job nearer to Mum. If only I didn't push her to hitting me, we'd be okay. Kim held herself well, so confident and bonny. Everyone mentioned we made a perfect couple and how romantic it was that we had 'gone out' as kids.

Our teenaged relationship had been short-lived, of course. I was a younger boy, and older Kim had found other boyfriends. I'd had girlfriends, too, of course, but most of the villagers remembered us being together.

I'd behaved cockily, I suppose, when I returned. You need to hold yourself confident like that as a man in my job, and Kim held her own in the confidence stakes too. She looked the part to walk alongside me, well-presented and attractive. The perfect power couple; Kim had seemed delighted with that.

It wasn't until later that her complaints built up. I needed to change this and that. I had to improve and lose weight. I'd got a bigger belly, my shoes looked ridiculous, and I needed to stand up straighter.

'What will people think?' mattered most to Kim. I went along with that. What people think matters. We had an image to maintain. We weren't like those others from the village. We did better, got promoted to a higher level. We did well for ourselves. We possessed the common

touch, but we behaved as if we were superior. We pointed out our car, our holidays. She kept herself slender. She could be mistaken for a twenty-three-year-old from behind.

One time, I dared to suggest that Kim should dress her age. There's a fine line between sexy older lady and mutton. I didn't say it like that, of course. I just mentioned that she should dress like a woman her age we were watching on TV. I shouldn't have said anything. My comment dropped like lead, and Kim exploded. 'I'm not dressing like that fuddy-duddy. Everyone says I look five years younger, maybe more. I'm not even middle-aged.'
'It's classy, no?'
'The minute you start dressing old, you are old.'
She hadn't changed her style much since the 1990s. She still lived that era in her head. At work, she power dressed, but at the weekend, her revealing outfits encouraged male attention. 'Gorgeous,' men said, after six pints from a distance.

I felt jealous, I admit that she loved every minute of the attention (and no doubt my jealousy). It gave her power. It fuelled her ego. I discerned that she was plotting her next move, not just one place ahead, but several moves in advance. From keeping up with the neighbours, to the politics of the tennis club, the rotary women meetings, and even church, Kim planned and plotted and made friends with the right people to gain extra for herself. She drew an opponent in, only to take them down a few moves later. She thought all of them most stupid, and her plans to outwit them all never ceased to amuse her. I wasn't much different, I suppose, at least on the surface.

I threw her a surprise birthday party, spending a lot of time sorting out arrangements on the sly. Even for most people, the secretiveness would be difficult, but with Kim, it built up to a monumental task.

I arranged a night out with her girlfriends, giving them the mission of delivering Kim to the party venue at the correct time. Kim agreed to the night out with no problem; she would have all her fans running around her. Jan, who was involved from the start, coordinated getting Kim from the wine bar to the hotel function room, where the event was to begin at 8 pm and later told me what had happened.

'Thank God for a night out,' Kim had apparently announced, saluting with her glass.

'Yeah, cheers Kim,' they all shouted.

'Hey, why don't we finish this one and go to the Imperial Hotel?' suggested Jan.

'Yeah, let's go,' Moya agreed.

'What? Now?' Kim whined. 'Why? We've just got here.'

'They've got two-for-one cocktails.'

'Okay, in a wee bit.'

Jan checked her watch and agreed.

'Yeah, later is fine.'

'Two drinks here, and then we'll go.' Sheona had nodded to Jan.

'Not yet, though.' Kim reportedly glanced at the door.

A while later, the debate about leaving continued. 'Come on, I think the half price offer only lasts until 9 pm,' suggested Moya.

'That's right,' another chipped in, as they finished second drinks.

'Okay. I'm away to the toilet,' Kim announced.

The girls got agitated as she spent an age in the toilet. It grew later and later.

'What's keeping her?' wondered Jan. 'Do you think she knows?'

Kim returned and sat down again.

'I thought we were going,' whined Sheona, already shrugging on her coat.

'One more drink,' announced Kim, already gesturing for another tray of drinks.

Jan downed her wine without a blink and stood up. 'Right, that's it. Let's go!'

'Sit down,' ordered Kim.

Jan said they all complied. Looking up, Kim had peered beyond her friends. 'Greg, how are you? Fancy meeting you here. Why don't you join us? It's my birthday.'

Back at the Imperial, Mum asked me, "What's going on?'

'I don't know, do I? She's not here,' I snapped.

'Where is she? I need the loo.'

'You can't go into the foyer. What if she sees you there?'

'She's an hour late.'

'They'll have been held up. Maybe it's a taxi issue, or they don't want to hurry her in case she becomes suspicious. She'll be here any second.' I started to wonder, though.

What if something had happened? Had she found out and was angry? She was always angry, no matter what I did. I'd have done something wrong again, for sure.

Her girlfriends eyed each other warily as Kim and her posse moved onto the venue. They trailed in behind her, embarrassed, unable to say anything as Kim strode into her own surprise party arm-in-arm with the man she was having an affair with.

She was furious—both with me and with her friends. She hated secrets —or other peoples' secrets, at least. Clearly, she loved her own. I had kept this secret from her and caused all of this humiliation.

Who's the guy?' Mum questioned. 'What's he doing out with her?' I tried to make excuses but could only muster up a mumbled, 'I don't know.' I did know, though, of course.

'It looks worse than it is,' babbled Jan.

Sheona, in particular, seemed upset.

'It was a last-minute thing, not like it was arranged or anything,' chipped in Moya. 'A chance meeting.'

'I thought she was out with her girlfriends,' Mum said.
'Maybe he counts as one of the girls,' suggested a cousin from over her shoulder.
'Oh, one of them gays,' said Mum.

FIFTY-FIVE

RHIANNON

I TAKE the chess notebook out with me when I walk. Often, I'll scribble notes about plans I can carry out to annoy Kim—small things, like she used to do to me at work. Just perplexing microaggressions that end up taking over her day and ruining it.

It's a Saturday today, so I can't visit the house. The neighbour's daughter visits on Saturdays.

When the accountants started Saturday morning shifts. During the week, I never showed up for work at the accountants until after Kim had opened the door and turned off the alarm. That meant not turning up until quarter to the hour at the earliest, as I didn't want to chance ruining her arrival. The first time I worked a Saturday, I showed up as normal, at my allocated time, giving Kim time to open up. I entered the back door and immediately heard the alarm fire off. I fumbled about in the dark, and then tore through the halls, finding my way. *She's not here like normal. Why? What the hell has happened?*

'Shit, shit, shit!' I panicked. I couldn't find the alarm, when I finally did my brain was blank. *What is the code? What is the code?'*

Kim always took charge of the alarm. The boss had shown me

how on the day of the interview. I remembered the shape, left to right and then down. 1 ... 2 ... 3 ... 6. The ringing stopped. I leant against the wall until I heard the front door open. I checked my watch. 8:50 am.

'What are you doing?' asked Kim.

'I heard the alarm,' I announced.

She stared at me as if I was an idiot.

'We all heard the alarm.' She stood with her arms folded, as if accusing me of something.

'I didn't let the alarm go off,' I offered. I breathed and smiled.

'I always open the door.' Kim huffed.

'I know. I thought you'd be here. You usually are by half-eight.'

'Not on a Saturday! We're starting later at the weekend. We aren't seeing anybody until 9:20, so I told everyone I'd be at the door at 8:50.'

She was precise, at least, and punctual. The gang arriving for work huddled around her, watching us talk, not rushing about their business. They had a ringside seat at the show early morning.

'Okay.' I shrugged. 'I didn't know.'

I figured it wasn't a big deal. I had only come in and turned off the alarm, but the littlest things could set Kim off.

'I told everyone that.'

She hadn't told me.

I made sure I turned up at 9 am every Saturday to allow her majesty the ceremonial opening of the door and turning off of the alarm.

Three months later, I turned up at 9 am and sensed a different atmosphere immediately. I opened the door to noise and a buzz about the place. I headed through to reception to witness staff and clients already sitting there waiting.

Kim glowered at me and indicated I should head to the back room. She brought a new girl with her; one I hadn't seen before.

'Where have you been? People are here already,' she growled in a stage whisper.

'Do we start on time now on a Saturday?'

'Yes,' the new girl chipped in.

'Who are you?' I barked.

'You don't know me. I don't know you either, but you seem like a terrible person. Is this the diva of the place, Kim? There's always one, eh?'

Kim laughed.

'This is Margo. She started this morning—great fun.' Kim's face darkened as she spun back to me. 'Anyway, people are waiting. It's totally unprofessional. I told everyone we were changing to usual hours on a Saturday from today.'

She hadn't told me.

FIFTY-SIX

RHIANNON

 I haven't returned to the garden or the fence for a while. It was time for some old-fashioned Scottish psychotherapy: I've taken hold of my senses, given myself a good shake, and got a grip.

I was committing trespass. Is that illegal in Scotland? I thought there was something about a right of way for ramblers. I wasn't rambling, though, more loitering about. It probably doesn't come under a right of way to skulk in people's gardens behind their shed after cutting planks in their fence.

Vandalism or destruction of private property might be the charge. 'Up to no good.' What I've been doing is surely not allowed, if not plain weird.

Am I going mad? No one would care anyway.

Most folks are living, working, paying for stuff, consuming, dying. They have no master plan like a Bond villain.

Politicians, perhaps, are up to something. Plotting and scheming is their job. No doubt they imagine we are all at it, too. That's why we are all being traced and tracked through our phones and what we buy.

I have of course, been up to something, but it's small fry. I'm not taking down corporations, or handing out lucrative contracts to my mates. I've simply been scratching a bit of wood near a park and lurking. Still, these things start small. Maybe the principle is similar, but I'm not doing it for personal gain. It's a compulsion, an itch to scratch—maybe even an addiction.

It wasn't an addiction when I started, but none are, are they? You don't become an alcoholic with just an initial sip. A like becomes a habit first, and then an addiction. There must be a cut-off point. You hear, 'He descended into addiction.' Like sliding down a slope. I believe it's more like an allergic reaction. One time you're fine; the second time, you've got it full-blown.

As my addiction progressed, I learnt their routine: when they'd leave, when they'd return. Kim's hours have been the same for years. Rob always left first, taking the car at 7:45 am to arrive at work at 8:30. It was only a half-hour drive, but he was one of those people who liked being early. Kim would leave on foot at 8:15 am, walking for 13 minutes to work and arriving with two minutes spare.

I'd seen her arrive and wait outside for those two minutes, waiting for her flunkeys to arrive in attendance before opening the door with a flourish like it was an event premiere. If she could have, her Imperial Highness would have cut a ribbon and pulled a string with a wee curtain to reveal a celebratory plaque.

At the height of my addiction, I stood for minutes, several days in a row, in the messy space between the shed and the fence. I got a kick out of that, although I had been fearful of authorities apprehending me. If caught, I'd be required to confess to my madness.

The first time I'd stepped out from the back of the shed, their dog jumped about in a frenzy at the conservatory window. I had jumped right back in place. I worried about leaving footprints on the grass, until I realised it was AstroTurf. I also worried about the dog. Conservatories can heat up. It might be like leaving the dog in a hot car. I peeped around to check. They had cracked open the top window to let in some air.

When I returned the next day, I took some food for the dog and shoved it in through the window. Then I sat in the garden, relaxed in the knowledge that no one could catch me. It took a while for me to achieve that level of comfort. But the fence lay behind me, the house in front and the house next door had no windows facing the garden. The other house, on the right belonged to the poor dear who couldn't reach the top floor.

A cat ambled by. 'Oh, they have a cat,' I thought, considering cutting off its collar to cause upset. But when I read the tag, the moggy did not belong to them. I lopped off some flower heads, as boredom set in, but decided to leave it at that. I decided I needed extra excitement to bother with this addiction much longer.

FIFTY-SEVEN

RHIANNON

 Last night I fell asleep on the couch again and slipped into that half asleep–half awake state. I could hear voices, people talking back and forth and the click of a walkie-talkie. Within moments, I fell into dreaming about my childhood home and the house across the road. Fire engine lights flashing. The chatter of the men on the radios.

I visualised the bustle: huge men barging about. Although normal-sized to me now, they were giants to a five-year-old. Again, I saw Kim, emotionless, clutching her bag in her hand, straight down as always. The noise became louder, the lights flashed brighter in front of my fluttering eyelids. I grew aware of my actual surroundings, in my flat with the window open. Opening my eyes, I followed the commotion to the window. An ambulance sat flashing outside. Someone had been knocked down at the traffic lights. 'Turn the light off,' one paramedic instructed the other.

Hi there

A Facebook message popped up from Rob.

Hello :-)

How are you?

I'm great, how about you?

I'm ok. Will you be at the home today?

I wasn't going to be, but I suppose I can be...

I'll be there later.

ok :-)

He unsent all the messages.

FIFTY-EIGHT

RHIANNON

I FANCY A MOAN, so the next day, I tell Mum how Sheona used to harass me.

'Wipe the dust from your feet, as they are nothing but a bunch of whoores and whooremaisters,' Mum announces, as if it is relevant to a current situation.

I laugh as if it's the first time I'd heard it.

'You smell of smoke,' Mum says.

I still have the bonfire smell on me and I realise I haven't washed that grey hoodie.

'Yeah, I was at a bonfire.'

'Is it November?'

I snort. It's not even close to Bonfire Night, and it's ridiculous that the acrid smell of smoke permeated my clothing as I hid behind a person's shed.

'She was there, at that fire,' Mum announces out of nowhere.

'Who?'

'Kim.'

'Oh?'

'Ah yes, she was outside right there with you.' She nods

knowingly even though we have been over this before. 'Everyone thought Alec did it. Maureen had a fling with your dad, and Alec caught them together in their house. I caught them, too.'

'My Auntie Nettie slapped her in the stair for that,' Mum added, which made her laugh.

'He killed Maureen in a jealous rage, I reckon. Escaped the fire himself. He must have thought Kim was in there too, but she was out with you, at the park.' She seems convinced. 'Of course, Maureen was a well-known whore, and he had a bad temper. Some family that! Her sister drowned off the pier at Blackpool—she was that drunk.'

Another nugget from the past.

'Alec never spoke about it at the club, but my he raged after drinks for nothing at all. Kim couldn't help being who she was, getting beaten by her father. He certainly hit her mother, although that woman always deserved a doing in my mind.'

On my way out, I spot Rob, and we sit for a while.

'We're making a habit of this,' I comment. I'd been making a habit of hanging around here so I could 'accidentally' meet him. The text messages were a recent addition.

Today's visit definitely had the air of an arrangement.

'Do you know what this place is missing?'

'What?'

'Decent coffee.'

Lesley rolls her eyes from the reception. I notice that Rob appears anxious.

'We should go for a coffee somewhere,' he mumbles.

'Yes, I'd love that.'

He slides me his number on a piece of paper, already written out.

'Best not communicate on Facebook.' He winks

'Okay.'

He's up to something, too. We've been arranging to be together, and now things need to be out of Kim's view. It's a different dynamic altogether.

FIFTY-NINE

ROB

Dear Diary,

Over the years, I became more and more dependent on her. I was like an attendant to a noble, required I prepare everything for my superior. My primary concern was pleasing Kim and following her regulations. I could not deviate from her plans.

Rules governed everything in our lives: which clothes to wear, how to wear them, how to serve dinner. If it wasn't agreeable to them—Bang! I got a blow to the head. Things had to be to her liking all the time. I did all in my power to follow her instructions, but I was still damned if I did, damned if I didn't.

When I did well, her wishes increased to an impossible level and the violence intensified. No matter what I did, there would be trouble. I tried to avoid upsetting her. I struggled, full of nerves, to second-guess her next move, until I was paralysed, unable to move at all. I didn't dare step out of line. I was incapacitated. Emasculated. I lived in fear, scared of being accused of being her abuser.

'I hope you die, you waste of space.' She screamed from the top of the stairs. Veins bulged in her neck as she pulled the glass mirror off the wall and hauled it down the stairs towards me.

'What the HELL?' I cowered away. When I stood up, she flung a stool. Then a shoe hit me on the arm as I protected my head.

'Have that and that,' she shouted, as each item was launched.

Terrified, I called the police. I stayed outside until they arrived, listening to her rampage around the house, tipping over tables and hurling ornaments. She could not attack me in full view of the neighbours. 'Bastard!' she screamed out the window.

The police separated us to question us. I noticed that scratches had appeared on her face—some new self-inflicted injury. We both told our stories.

'Any more trouble here tonight, and one of you is going to be in the lock-up,' the officer said, and then left.

Kim had clearly lied about the violence, and the policeman probably believed her, based on her lacerations. That was the only explanation I had for her not being arrested immediately. Not twenty minutes later, as I bent down to pick up the shards of broken mirror, she ran at me and kicked me in the head. 'You!' was her only utterance, as I fell. Then she charged into the bedroom, slamming the door.

I pulled myself up, crawled to the car, and drove myself to hospital. I told everything to the doctor who examined me. With letting it all out, I felt unburdened, relieved, despite my burst ear drum and broken cheekbone. The doctor would have to report it, and I gave his consent.

I ventured home, slept on the couch, and called in sick to work the next day, too bruised and too tired to face my colleagues.

Later that day, the domestic violence unit phoned. I answered, thinking the doctor must have reported my injuries and this was the follow-up. To my surprise, they asked to speak to Kim. I handed her the phone but listened to the call on the phone in the bedroom.
'Are you okay? Do you want a social worker there? Just contact us if it happens again, and we'll arrest your husband,' I heard.
I stood there, looking at my bruised face in the mirror, accused of being the perpetrator. What she told police, I never found out. My legs felt numb, my knees gave way, and I dropped to the floor devastated. My heart sunk to the bottom of the ocean, lost and alone.

She was still on the call when I slouched down the stairs to the hall. 'Uh-huh, yeah, yeah,' I heard. Her simpering voice changed to say, 'I've got you now,' as soon as she hung up the phone. The words chilled me to the bone. She barged past to the kitchen. I winced, so scared I was fixed to the spot. Forcing myself to unglue my feet, I then ran back upstairs to retrieve a bag.

On returning downstairs, I spun to try to catch her, ready to pounce, but she was not there. Unsure what she would do next, I knew it would not be pleasant. I needed to escape. She could attack at any time, claiming self-defence. She rushed at me at the bottom of the stairs, preventing me from exiting. 'I'm going,' I said, still feeling the need to inform her of my every move.

'I don't think so, mister.' She threw herself at me, forcing me back onto the steps, attacking my face. I managed to cover myself, but not before she scratched my cheeks and neck. She backed off, huffing and puffing with the effort, which surprised me.

I paused, sprawled on the stair. She glared at me, her face purple with rage, her eyes filled with hate. A grin appeared on her face, although her eyes did not change. 'Do you know how stupid you are?'
I ignored the insult.

'Do you realise how many men I've had?'
My face and lips never moved.
'And you couldn't even work it out, or even say anything?'
I blanked it all.
'You are so dumb. So pointless.'
With tears running down my face, I finally wrestled her out of the way
to the door. Turning, she then charged back into the kitchen. I fled the
door and ran to the shed. She followed, frying pan in hand.

I believed this was the day I would die, but instead she shouted, 'Give
me your phone.' I watched as she smashed it into a hundred pieces.
'Don't you ever call the police on me again,' she hissed.

Everything in my life is back to front. 'You are abusive' means 'I am
abusive'. 'You are a bad person' means 'I am a bad person'. 'You hate
me' means 'I hate you'.

One night, I tried to persuade her to open up to me, to figure out what
was wrong with our relationship. As she always did, she blanked me.
She sat gazing ahead, her lips tight, refusing to say a word. Then she
whispered, 'Nobody understands what's in me.' I remember feeling
something chilling in that. I took my turn to stare in silence. I sensed
something evil inside her, something she was referring to.

She had a secret life of affairs, stealing money, lying, cheating people.
She lived that way, acted that way, and I experienced it. However, not
until she told me she was a wicked person, did it dawn on me that it
was actually the truth. How can I be so surprised at how she acts,
when she told me to my face how bad she was? My gut had sensed it
for years, but I had refused to believe it.

I'll always blame myself for not listening well enough.

SIXTY

RHIANNON

 Yesterday, a ghost returned to haunt me at work.

The phone in my office rang. 'Hi, Rhiannon. You have a phone call from some angry woman. I don't know what she's on about. I tried to placate her, but she was determined to speak to you. A wee warning, she sounds mad. A ... Sheona Work.'

'Okay, put her through.'

She did, and without any introduction, Sheona Work began, 'Hi, Rhiannon. I had to call you.'

'Okay, can I ask what this is about?'

'I've had a new client in, and she showed me your work, work you've done previously. It's not up to standard. I had to call and let my feelings be known.'

I sat down. 'What? Who are you?'

Rather than answer my question, she continued, 'I'll have to report this to a higher authority.'

My stomach lurched.

'Who?' I thought. 'God, surely not ICAS?

'I don't appreciate people like you in our accountancy line of work. It's totally unprofessional.'

A bell rang in my mind. 'Thanks for your input. Must go. Bye-bye.'

Later, I spoke to the boss about it. 'Do you know a Sheona Work?'

'Yeah. Used to be Sheona McPherson. Right pain in the arse.'

Kim's pal Sheona had returned, raging at me again. God, I couldn't escape the woman. But why now?

Is Kim thinking about me like I'm thinking about her? Have I pricked her memory, causing her to tell Sheona to harass me again? Or is she simply friends with another bully like herself—birds of a feather and all that.

Perhaps I'm as terrible as they are now. They made me adopt their dreadfulness in order to survive their pecking order.

The fact someone had married Sheona surprised me enough, but then I had to wrap my head around that she'd held a grudge for twenty-five years.

So, not only me.

I need to up my game.

SIXTY-ONE

RHIANNON

AFTER ABOUT A MONTH of visiting the garden, today I spied that the small window by the back door had been left cracked open. I struggled to reach in and fiddle with the catch for the door, which clicked and the door opened.

The dog began barking but licked me once he realised I was no threat. I'm the friendly garden person who gives him food, after all. I rewarded him with treats from my pocket. I checked his collar. Scooter—stupid name for a dog.

I found myself in a room off the conservatory, the utility room. Even Kim's laundry was magazine-liveable perfect. The clothes were separated into dirty and clean and folded into piles ready to be put away. The outdoor shoes were lined up in order, both wellies and the ones for doing the garden in. A grey plaque hung on the wall and read, '*Smile—while you still have teeth.*' She's got plenty. She's like the Cheshire cat with her mouthful of gnashers.

Then I spotted the hooks holding the spare keys. I tried them all in the back door until I found the spare key for that entrance and pocketed it. *Would they miss it?* Unlikely.

I passed through to the conservatory and peered into the immaculate kitchen. I sighed. Has she a cleaner?

Needing to meet with Jan, I cut my visit short.

SIXTY-TWO

RHIANNON

'I TELL YOU, I'M NO' happy. Terry is on a diet—we both are but he's lost way more than me. It's infuriating, He tells me I'm fat and I'm lucky to have him. His body is getting smaller, but his big bawheid is getting bigger. Thinks he's Tom Hardy. I told him his teeth are shit, and since he lost weight, his arse is flat but he still has a pot belly. It's like he put his body on backwards, so he needn't think he's the catch of the day.' She pauses to sip her drink.

'How are you getting on at work?' I ask.

'Och, all right. I'm picking up the boss tonight, ha ha. It's more a favour for Kim. They've been away the weekend.'

'I didn't see anything on Facebook,' I say, and then bite my tongue. I almost gave away my stalking.

'Oh, they don't put anything on Facebook in case they get robbed. Someone could break in.'

I gasp, but cover it with a cough. 'Something in my throat,' I squeak out.

'Ha ha. I hate that, nearly choking on your own saliva. Yeah, they been away a wee mini break. Left on Friday for London. Flying back tonight. I've been feeding Scooter, their dog, as they don't want it to go to a kennel.'

My eyes widen. I could have met her in there. 'When are you picking them up?'

'I pick them up at 8 pm.'

After Jan goes, I check the flights. Sure enough, I spot a London flight due in at 7:45 pm. That gives them time to pick up their bags, exit, and meet Jan. By my calculations, they won't return to the house until 8:30 pm. It's 4 pm now. I dash into the cobblers.

'Can you cut a spare key for me?'

He glances at his watch. 'You just made it,' he says. He wants to shut up shop, so he does the job very quickly.

SIXTY-THREE

RHIANNON

I RETURN to Kim's with the copied key and replace the spare.

I scan the kitchen. 'What can I do to annoy her?' I wonder out loud to the dog.

As I think, I notice socks in the drying basket. Out of habit, I pair them while I think. I pull out and pocket three random socks; she'll never find the companions to the ones left. I doubt she'll notice right away. If her life is anything like mine, these things disappear anyway. I pick out two more designer socks. *These might be missed.*

I remove the remote control for the TV from its holder and hide it in the shed. As I make my way back in, I scoop up some dog shit they missed from the garden and place it in the centre of Kim's kitchen.

She used to work with small inconveniences, small irritations. Small things can ruin a whole day. Tiny nuisances can slowly steal your joy as much as devastating deaths or ill health. You expect those; they are part of life. A smooth-running boring day can still be contented. Disruption is ... well ... disrupting. Running late, missing the train, your water bottle lid falling off in your bag, a train ticket left on the kitchen table, standing on a building brick, too many of those stressful irritations can tip you over the edge.

I rarely feel bad about doing those things; at the time, I feel excited. But after I leave, I experience a feeling that started back when I worked with her. I don't understand why. but I find myself doing strange, impulsive things that make no sense to others but perfect sense to me. When adrenaline kicks in, I become a 'flighter' because I fear the 'fighter' in me.

Once, when Kim had poked me one time too many, I ran out of work tired and stressed. I left the building and found myself in the car park, gasping for breath. A passing friend asked me if I felt okay, and I realised I couldn't breathe. I couldn't say more than two words. I made no sense at all.

Now, people might call it a panic attack, but back then, I just headed home and lay down until it passed. I got in so much trouble for that from Kim.

After visiting their house, I sometimes feel like that—more out of breath than I should be from the walk alone. It builds up, escalating from the time I leave Kim's house to the time I reach my flat in a crescendo of heart-racing breathlessness.

SIXTY-FOUR

ROB

Dear Diary,

Like anyone, I experience stress, but I don't face it. I cram mine down and suffocate it until the brick of what I am dealing with adds to a wooden block tower of stress. I cope well on the surface. Then ... one brick too many and the whole tower comes tumbling down.

I'm hoping that, by continuing to write, I can move on from this hell I am living. I feel a catharsis in writing it all down ... until regret kicks in. While writing my journal, I have been reflecting on what I should have done and when should I have done it.

Hundreds of questions about my character ripple to the surface in ugly, grasping waves. In response, armed with the knowledge of hindsight, I wonder If only I'd done this, or that. What hindsight doesn't give me is the means to deal with the present, where I live.

Domestic abuse from a female to a male is a taboo subject. It leads some to consider a man weak; that he possesses no strength of character. I pride myself in knowing that, despite it all—despite the personal threats, the emotional verbal and physical attacks—I only ever raised my hand one solitary time and never followed through. Kim just laughed and hit me again and again.

I genuinely bear her no ill will. I do not love her—that died with the heaviness of my heart, if it ever existed at all.

We tried counselling in an attempt to find a place to negotiate. During our single session with a counsellor, I realised that making this relationship work appeared hopeless.
'What problems, in your own words, would you say you two have, Rob?'
I hesitated. 'Well, I do everything. Kim has certain rules, and when I don't follow them, she attacks me. Sometimes she attacks me for no reason. She has affairs, runs up massive debts, which I pay off, and lies continually.'
It was a heavily edited answer.
Kim stared forwards, making no eye contact with me or the counsellor. The counsellor paused and turned to Kim. 'What do you think is wrong with this relationship?'
She considered it for a minute and answered, 'Nothing at all.'

I should have walked out right then, but I didn't due to fear and conditioning. I'd been programmed to stay static. On the way home, I sat in silent terror in the car. Kim sat stony-faced.

At home, she complained, 'You made me out to be a bitch.'
'Well, you are ... sometimes you are.' The words slipped out.
'How dare you?' she spat.
Exasperated, I didn't care what she said. She always exploded, however I behaved. 'We don't have a relationship. We have a dictatorship.'
'What are you talking about?'

'You tell me to do things, and I do them ... or else.'

She stood over me. 'If you don't want to do something, you shouldn't do it.' She hissed.
'I'm too scared not to.'
She threw her head back and guffawed. 'Some man you are. Why don't you leave, then?'
'I'm too scared to do that too, or too stupid.'
She looked both shocked and offended that I dared to stand up to her.

I didn't sleep that night at all. I lay awake, terrified I might not wake up otherwise.

SIXTY-FIVE

RHIANNON

 It is too late to back out now. I'm in deep, so deep that I must continue, or what was the point in starting?

If they find the hatch now, it will all have been for nought. I have no way of knowing whether Kim is even perplexed by the small things I do to annoy her.

I see her now and then, but she seems no different. No one even noticed my doings. Most people were just getting on with their lives. Whole burglaries occur and no one sees anything. Massive pieces of equipment disappear. Cars are stolen, and no one ever sees them getting driven off. People aren't that observant.

I sometimes believe I'm the only person in the world going around noticing the moves people make, wondering what their purpose is.

Today, I popped too much salt into Kim's curry, which was cooling on the hob. I've graduated from the kitchen, the conservatory, and utility room into the living room. I've visited almost every day over the past month, conjuring up annoying irritations. Sometimes, I hide things, like a magazine under a cushion. On other occasions, I sit cross-legged on their floor, contemplating ideas.

How about fish? I'd read about someone putting seafood in curtain poles and behind radiators, and folk couldn't find the cause of the terrible smell and ended up selling their houses because of it. Some even had to take a reduced price due to the fish smell, which suggested an electrical problem. No, I needed something that had no explanation.

Once, I defrosted the freezer. I debated unplugging it, but I decided instead to switch it off at the wall. Unplugging would appear too deliberate. Switched off could be accidental. Someone perhaps aimed for an adjacent switch or it was tripped during cleaning. I imagined the arguments about who let the freezer defrost.

Another time, I left a tap on. I covered the plughole with a plate and left the tap running slow.

My most extravagant ploy came when I spotted Kim's new work shoes, still in the box. I took a photo of them and bought an exact copy in a smaller size. Then I replaced the left one with the smaller version I had bought. That would ruin her day. And if she ever took them back to the shop, what an inconvenience. I could imagine the row.

Today, I also moved upstairs into their bedroom.

I sat at her dressing table and applied her lipstick. Then I snapped it from its stalk and pressed the lid back on hard. The next time she applies it, it will fall right off, with any luck onto her perfect white shirt. I spotted some jewellery boxes and opened them to try the pieces on me. A pair of sapphire earrings called to me. One went into my back pocket. I left the box open to make sure she misses it.

The time before last, my itching powder ended up in her shoe; this time, it goes on her pillow. I sniffed their pillows to establish who slept where. Rob's aftershave matched the pillow on the left.

This whole carry-on is leaving me empty. I had a thrilling feeling to begin with. But my excitement is diminishing, and I can't see the results. They might not have noticed any of these things, or perhaps they dismiss them as things that don't matter. Perhaps they are happy-go-lucky types, the opposite of me. Today, I decided not to return, to leave them alone. However, on my way out, I performed a final, spur-of-the-moment action. A reaction will be guaranteed.

SIXTY-SIX

ROB

Dear Diary,

How will I leave? I'd love to say that I will pluck up the courage, shove my pride aside, leave her and set up home in my parent's old house. I'll stay there this time. I should take time to heal myself, to attend counselling, work on my confidence and become self-aware. I should find confidence in my solitude, perhaps find some retreat or other.

But it is not like that. It is ending. I have met someone else. I don't understand why I find it so easy to speak to her, but I do. I know she will understand me.

I sense that if I tell her everything and explain the problem, she will help me. I sense it in my heart. This person, while only existing in my life for a short time, has given me the strength to leave. I am indebted to her more than any other.

Rhiannon has opened my eyes to what a normal woman can be, not threatening and fear-inducing. Kim mentioned seeing her on Facebook and told me Rhiannon used to try to boss her around. I'd snorted at that. Kim said she refused to allow Rhiannon's bossiness and put her in her place. I bet she did—the same way she put me in mine.

Rhiannon seems so gentle and quiet, so understanding of how Kim acts. It made me question whether Rhiannon might have experienced Kim's evil side too, the part that her other friends either did not notice or overlooked. It drew me to Rhiannon even further.

It started as a passing acquaintance, until it grew and I sensed she must have felt the same as I did. Last week at the care home, I touched her hand, and she didn't recoil.

On Saturday night, I told Kim I did not love her anymore because of her violence. I realised I don't love her, since I have those feelings for another woman—a woman who would never hurt me. She seems so kind, so sweet. She makes me envision another life.

I don't remember too much after telling Kim the truth. But I remember the relief, even as the punches and kicks rained down on me. I had resigned myself to one last beating.

Kim must have sensed she had lost her power over me. She soon gave up, ran out and drove off.

I'd had enough. I couldn't live like this anymore. I had to leave her forever. I need to stop all this writing now. I've found it does not help me. I must consider the future instead, one step at a time. I can't move backwards, only forwards. I need to leave it all in the past, to deal with this once and for all.

SIXTY-SEVEN
RHIANNON

'ARE YOU OKAY?' I ask.

Rob seems forlorn as I chat with him at the home after visiting Mum. It's become our regular thing now.

'It's Kim.' He runs his fingers over his head.

'Yes,' I say in acknowledgment, but give nothing away, like I'm playing poker. When I ask after her, he continues. 'She's stressed right now but doing okay.'

I can't imagine her being stressed. She is always in control.

Is he being vague on purpose? Does he want me to ask more? Maybe he thinks we're friends.

He changes the subject. 'I'm going away for work straight from here. I've a conference in Liverpool.'

'You'll miss her?' I drag the subject back to her.

'No,' he declares staring straight at me. 'I'll be fine to get away ... things aren't great.' He is verging on crying, which makes me elated.

I dare to reach out and touch his hand, like he had mine another time.

'She is a nightmare. You wouldn't believe.'

'I believe it. She bullied me too.'

'She did?' His shoulders lift. 'I thought so. She hinted at putting you in your place, but I thought she only acted that way with me.' He glances up as Lesley passes, perhaps nosing around at our conversation, noticing us getting closer and disapproving of us doing that in her old folks' home.

'Can we get out of here? Not publicly—it's dangerous,' he whispers.

'Dangerous?'

'Maybe back to your flat.'

'I ... I can't just now,' I stammer.

'Of course, you are busy.' He deflates.

'Another time for sure,' I suggest, and his shoulders lift again.

'Yes, that would be great'

I can't take him to the flat now, however much I want him. And I want him badly.

I rush home. *I've gone too far this time*, I think, as I stare at Scooter sitting in my living room. I took him with no bother. He trusts me now, but I can't take any more chances. I'm guilty of dognapping. *Is that a huge crime?*

I lessen my culpability in my mind. I just captured him for a while, borrowed him even. Rob will be attending his conference this weekend, so he won't discover the dog is missing. Kim will have that pleasure.

As for my plan not to visit the house again? Well, that didn't last long. Of course, I have to return. I have to take the bloody dog back.

SIXTY-EIGHT
RHIANNON

 Yesterday, Kim posted on the Facebook town pages a post that read 'Missing dog' with a photo of Scooter. I added a quick care emoji and commented 'Hope the dog comes back soon X.' He licked my hand after I did it.
  I messaged Rob about it.

Hi, I see the dog is missing!!!

              Kim is up the wall.

I bet. (*Good news!*)

              I'm in Liverpool still

Love Liverpool great city <3

              How are you?

I'm ok. It's weird. I miss you. X

Can I have your number, you never called me on mine :(

Ok.

Great, I'll call you later. I'll be back in 2 days x

I'll look forward to it x

I'll be in to see Mum at the usual time x

I'll keep an eye out for the dog. X

SHE WILL HAVE *his Facebook login details, but no access to his phone while he is away. Rob could get away with this interaction, based on the dog situation, but again, he quickly deleted the messages. All the while, the pooch sat on the couch with me.*

Scooter barked. I hoped my neighbours couldn't hear.

I decided to turn the radio on low, which might disguise the dog noise. I might be dog-sitting for a friend if barks emanated from my flat. Also, sometimes it is difficult to pinpoint where the noise comes from: the barks could be coming from outside.

SIXTY-NINE

RHIANNON

I MUST MAKE sure I return the dog by the time Rob gets home from his conference. I've toyed with the idea of just replacing Scooter in his bed in the shed or shoving him in the garden, as though he ran away and simply returned.

Earlier, I panicked at the idea they might search for a gap in the fence Scooter could have escaped from and find my hinges. They might have done that, if I hadn't cleverly left the side gate open when I left with him, so they would focus on that as his mode of escape. There'll be blame on either side for leaving the latch off. For all my compulsive behaviour with the last-minute grabbing of the dog, I still planned on the spot. I was quite proud of that.

I decide Scooter should be placed back in his bed. There might even be accusations of her making up the whole event for attention. *Sure, one minute the dog was gone, and then it's there again like magic,* Rob might scoff.

I giggle at the idea of creating tension between them.

SEVENTY

RHIANNON

TWO DAYS after I spoke to Rob, I sit on their bed.

This is where he sleeps.

I lie on his pillow and smell him. A whiff of aftershave I recognise immediately.

I need Rob souvenirs. I don't know whether I love him or if he loves me, but I want him. I want him, and I want her not to have him. I want to capture something, take something from her and possess it myself.

He once fancied me enough to give me a Valentine's Day card, before she stole him away, so there is a chance he could be mine.

They own his and hers wardrobes. I raid his. I find a jumper with three large buttons at the collar. I remember him wearing it the first time I met him in the home. I cut the top button off and pull some fluff off the sleeve. It must not bother him, but it bothers me. *Why don't people remove the lint from their jumpers?*

I replace the jumper at the back of the cupboard. He'll find it one day and wonder what happened to the button. I hope Kim turns the place upside down looking for it.

I still want her upset. I rip a sleeve off a shirt of hers at the back of the wardrobe, too, one she might not see for a long time. They own a whole shoe cupboard, all laid out in smart racks. The walking boots at the back I imagine wouldn't be used much; they might not notice those missing for months. Later, it might niggle if his matching boot can't be found, so I swipe one. Knowing her, she'd shout at him for being stupid enough to lose a whole boot. It was bound to cause friction.

More and more, I want him and things that belong to him: his possessions, his smell, any part of him I can own. I spot his comb with hair entangled in it. It's not an inconvenience for either of them, but it's a memento for me.

I own a whole piece of that lovely boy's hair, just for me.

ROB APPEARS at my door minutes after I return from his house. The main door to the stair is broken, so I had no need to buzz him in. He gave me no warning at all. My heart pounds.

This is the day I have been dreading. I expect him to say he had seen me and demand, 'What the hell are you doing?'

My backpack with all my souvenirs from his property still sits in the hall, so I have no defence.

Instead, he says, 'Hi,' and shifts his feet

'Hi? What ...?' My mouth feels dry as sand.

'I needed to see you. Don't you want to see me?'

I blink and lie, 'Well, yes.' He seems like that boy again, not a man in his fifties.

'I've left her,' he says, stepping towards me.

I hold him tight. My anxiety builds up into jangling nerves, and then excitement, and before I know it, I'm kissing him. There's something so sexy about knowing what I was doing earlier, and now him being here, almost catching me. The fact that he wants me too intoxicates my entire body.

All of it happens out of my control. I didn't recognise how much I longed for human company—not pity because I am lonely, but actual, physical touch. Pity from him would be the highest form of insult. I don't want him to feel concern for me. I want him to care, of course, but for me, not for my sadness.

It's taken me all this time to realise how much my loneliness has hurt me.

I am being set free.

He wants me for me.

SEVENTY-ONE

RHIANNON

HE HAS BEEN HERE three days. He maintains that he walked out because he had had enough. We went to bed that night and never lifted our heads for two days before hunger took over. He has many missed calls and furious texts from Kim; he showed me.

He told me terrible stories about how she treated him. My revenge feels justified now, and all I can think of is helping her victim, her husband. I have ended up being the noble hero for my actions—his female knight in shining armour.

'Why didn't you leave her before?'

'I left her many times. I had many turning points. I had a headache and stomach ache one day. I should have been heading straight to a chemist, but that wasn't possible because she had my daily journey home mapped out to the last detail. She expected me home at a certain time. I was too scared to go off track and turn up late. Can you imagine what that's like?' His face contorts in pain and disbelief at how he allowed it all to happen.

'Living in fear, yes. With her, absolutely yes.'

'So I decided not to go home—ever again.'

'But you did. Why?'

'She had me disbelieving my own feelings. I avoided what my gut knew until it shouted at me *This feels wrong!* and I still blanked it. I let my head and my heart override my intuition by looking for concrete evidence.'

'You had plenty of red flags,' I challenge him.

'Red flags become paranoia when you have been gaslit to that extent.'

'Gaslit?'

'Yes, she would deny anything was happening. She would say black was white and refuse to accept otherwise.'

'Such as?' He lists her sayings.

'I never said that. I didn't say that. You said that. That didn't happen. You imagine things. You're crazy. I never hit you. I didn't really hurt you. I didn't have an affair.'

'She had affairs?' I butt in, unsurprised.

'Yes, right in front of me.'

I nod. 'And you allowed that?'

He shakes his head at his own stupidity.

'I would have had to literally catch them in bed together to believe she was cheating. I was so brainwashed. Even then, she would deny it.'

'Do you think she is evil?'

'Everything she did was a lie designed to manipulate. But even if I did everything she forced me into doing, she would find some way for it to be wrong, to punish me. She had full control. I was too scared to do anything at all'

His head sinks down, and I hand him a drink and sit next to him. I want to understand him, but also her. 'Why was she like that, do you think?'

'Her dad abused her.'

'Oh?'

'Or she said he did. He probably did. I have no reason to disbelieve her, but with so many lies, it is hard to decipher the truth, you know?'

'Do you think that makes sense of it all? I don't understand what she gets out of being the way she is.' I tell him about my experiences with her, and it feels great to have someone listen, but today is my turn to pay attention.

'It's about power and domination, like her dad with her. She's repeating what he taught her. That must be the only way she knows.'

'Why did you not give up on her straight away?' I continue the interview.

'The manipulation didn't happen all at once. It crept in like an invisible virus that took over every part of me.' He falls onto my chest, and I hold him again.

'How was your sex life?' It was all I had to say to arouse him and lead him into bed again.

'She used sex as a weapon. She'd withdraw affection, mainly to act as puppeteer of my emotions, to unsettle me.'

It bothers me that he wanted to have sex with her, so I focus his attention back to me for a while. But I can't let my favourite subject go. 'She seemed so popular. I thought I was the problem.'

'She could act charming to people's faces; mostly to get what she wanted. Sex, or people to do things for her, or social climbing. She mocked people behind their backs. Everyone was mad who didn't share her interests in her head. She'd mock anyone she spotted in the lagoons, birdwatchers, artists. Anyone who did anything she didn't do was stupid.'

'Was she ever sorry? '

'Ha! She said those words, but if she really was, she'd have had to take responsibility and try improving herself. In her mind, there was no need to do that. She'd say sorry if you took offence after a hurtful remark. You see, my reaction was the issue. She'd say I'd driven her to assaulting me; her reaction was never the problem.'

'You looked like you had the perfect life, house, car, money, holidays.'

'She never had any money. She spent and spent and didn't care. She racked up thousands on credit cards. I bailed her out so many times, I could have bent over backwards fulfilling every one of her demands. I was never appreciated, just taken advantage of for what I provided. Our whole relationship was a game she had to win.'

I'd never be like that, I think, as I fall back into bed with my captive.

AFTERWARDS, I slip out of bed to shower as Rob sleeps on. As I towel my hair dry, I hear him banging about in the bedroom. When I slip out of the bathroom, he makes me jump. He is standing, waiting on me, his face drained of blood. In one hand, he holds a single sapphire earring, and in the other, a black-and-white checked scarf.

'What the hell is this?' he shouts. 'What's going on?'

SEVENTY-TWO

RHIANNON

'WHAT IS THIS?' he repeats.

'A scarf.' I state the obvious. I want to pass him, but he blocks my way.

'And this?'

'An earring.'

'Whose earring? Whose scarf?'

I feel a tightness in my stomach. 'I need to get dressed,' I mumble as I push past him.

He holds it aloft. 'It's Kim's earring! She went mad looking for it.'

I get a pang of satisfaction that she was annoyed, though it was not the plan for Rob to find out.

'How did you get it? It was in our bedroom, in a box on her sideboard.'

'I found the scarf tied to a lamppost.' I tell the truth about that at least.

'And ...' He held the earring up again.

I hesitate. 'I found the earring ...' I sounded less certain about that.

'This earring? You found this earring? I turned the house upside-down for the bloody earring. She blamed me for meddling in her sideboard. She'd not worn earrings for ten years, as her lobes had healed up. She couldn't have worn them out. She noticed it had gone because the box was opened. They were a gift from me years ago.'

I inwardly cursed myself for leaving the box open, but I'd wanted her to notice one had gone. Come to think of it, I couldn't remember her wearing earrings. I'd never checked that.

'Oh, I didn't know,' I muttered, finding no way out. I felt annoyed. *What was he looking for anyway? No, I can't blame him. He found out my secret.*

No wonder he searched for clues after living with her for all those years.

'How did you find it?' I whisper.

'I was looking for a phone charger. I thought there might be a spare one lying around that might fit my phone.'

Maybe that was true or maybe he was snooping.

'Never mind that. Why is it here?'

'I ... I wanted to get back at her... You know what she is like.'

'And?'

I pause. 'I broke into the house.'

He sits slumped on the bed with the items still in his hands.

'I don't know why. I realise it sounds mad,' I blurt out. I explain more, missing things out and dressing it up a bit so I don't sound so crazy. 'I lost my mind I guess.'

'You broke into our house. What?' He stops. 'Are you with me for me? Or...'

'Yes, I'm with you for you.'

'... to get back at her?' He finishes his sentence.

'It started as her.' It was all her, all revenge, and he was the pawn in my great chess game. Then it changed. I saved him. I became the real queen, a hero. 'I never knew I cared about you until later.'

If he doesn't want me now, there is nothing I can do. I can't take it all back. He knows what she was like. He knows she deserved it.

'Please, I was fixated by her. You know yourself she makes you mad. Makes you do things you wouldn't, question your own sanity.' I sound insane.

I must be mad. It is obvious I am nuts. I invaded another person's house and stalked and stole their husband. Where did that come from?

Mum keeps talking about the past: my grandmother and hers, all their doings.

Did they creep under my skin when I read their journals? Is it in my genes? Marie Riordan. Irene. Annie. Mum. Me. We are all one, and we cannot fight it. We can't be anything other than the sum of our history. Our blood mixed with our circumstances. Or has the murder flat had more of an influence on me than I thought?

Rob holds his head in his hands. The items lie on the bed beside him.

'Have I ever been bad to you?' I blurt.

'No. But you lied.'

'I didn't lie.'

'No, you didn't lie. You broke into my house, used me as a dupe to get at her.'

'No.'

'Yes! I'm a puppet in your game of revenge.'

'No,' I lie again, because he was. But things changed. 'It wasn't like that. I like you—love you,' I stumble on.

'I've heard that before.' He seems calmer. 'Do you not think she told me she loved me a million times? I've heard that phrase so many times it means nothing to me now. It doesn't even break the skin. It just bounces off. I'm numb to those words.'

He marches out of the room, and I hear him on the phone.

I am correct in assuming he was calling her. 'What did she say?'

'Nothing much. I didn't tell her what you did. I told her that I made a mistake. She told me to move back in. After all, she is my wife. At least I understand where I am.'

'Are you kidding me? After all you said about her? You can't go. You can't reject me again.'

'Again?'

'Like before, when we were young, in the shop.' I am frantic.

'What are you talking about?'

'And in the pub, you chose her.' I am so angry, the pain of his rejection all over again feels too hard to bear. Surely Colin rejecting me had shown I was meant to be with Bertie, the boy with the card.

It had come full circle, but here he was, leaving me and going back to her again.

SEVENTY-THREE
RHIANNON

 He has gone. He could be back with her already. He was with me en passant only. I hope that is not true. I hope he thinks better of walking out on me.

I'm not worse than her, am I?

He has returned to her, and maybe he will tell her I was stalking her. Why would he do such a thing?

SEVENTY-FOUR

RHIANNON

I SHOWER as hot as I can, drink a bottle of wine, and lie in bed fully clothed. I wake curled up in a ball with the covers wrapped around me like a knot.

'I'm sorry,' I say out loud, reaching over to no one there. I must have said it a thousand times before I fell asleep. I am not sure why I wake up, perhaps the booze. My eyes are nipping. I blink and blink again, and rub my eyes, which are stinging. *Is this just tiredness?* I head to the toilet and turn on the light. Things are hazy. I cough.

I can't see so well.

Is it smoke? I didn't leave a pizza in the oven, did I?

Then I hear the smoke alarm. I wake up fully.

'Shit the flat is on fire,' I say aloud, as I open the hall door to a corridor thick with smoke. I scream, cough, and the sprinklers spring into action.

I close the bedroom door. I grasp there is no way out into the hall to the door and down the stair. The doors are all fire doors, thank God, so I throw the duvet at the bottom of this one, in case further smoke gets in. I open the window and decide on climbing out.

I can escape somehow, I think. I scan the road below and shout for help. I climb out to the ledge, but wisps of smoke follow me out now. I struggle for breath as blue lights illuminate the night. A ladder comes up, and I'm lifted down and transferred to a stretcher.

'I'm asthmatic,' I cough, as they place an oxygen mask on me. I spot a woman in the alley, hand by her side, holding a bag straight down, staring at the fire in front of her. I'd recognise that anywhere. She watches the drama unfold in some sort of a trance.

I close my eyes and I am back in the village, watching the fire in 1976. This time, I watch on from behind, out of my body. I see small me holding the hand of a figure mesmerised by the fire consuming her mother and siblings. I remember holding Kim's right hand, and the smell and heat of the fire on my face. Her wee bag, held straight down as usual, was in her left hand. No, no, not a bag. Something metal—a canister, a container, a rusty red metal container. A jerry can.

It was a petrol can held straight down.

I open my eyes to the same alley. It's a can there, too. I try to speak, but I hiss instead, and my eyes close.

Where was Alec? Her dad stands there, as I remembered him before. He stumbles out the back door, only this time I remember his words, 'Kimberly, what have you done?'

I open my eyes. I repeat the phrase in a whisper before my eyes close and all goes black.

SEVENTY-FIVE
RHIANNON

I WAKE up in the hospital with dread and the effects of smoke inhalation. I realise I am in a bad way when the police come to speak to me without waiting for me to be released to recover at home.

'We believe it was arson,' announces the lady police officer. I grunt in acknowledgment and cough again.

'But we have questions. How would they have got into the stair? Could it be someone with a key?'

'That main door has never been fixed,' I explain. *Some police work,* I think, surely the police entered the stairway without a key.

'We are under the impression someone shoved a petrol-soaked rag through your letter box.'

I nod. My lack of expression, with no surprise, I can explain. I feel ill and exhausted.

'Who would do such a thing?' she asks.

I knew who could have done it, but it was not time to mention the figure in the alley just yet. I gave them a snippet to think about.

'I think I remember seeing someone, but it's all a bit hazy.' I wheeze.

'It would be great if you could give us anything, someone who might have a grudge against you, or if you saw anything unusual. '

'I'm so tired. I don't know for sure. But, like I say, I thought I saw someone, a woman outside across the road.'

That was enough. It had to wait. I must escape this stalemate and be free. It's essential that I leave the hospital to sort it all out, to reach the endgame.

SEVENTY-SIX

RHIANNON

BACK IN THE FLAT, I can see the damage is mainly smoke-related in the hall and water damage from the sprinklers. The police let me in but suggest I stay in a bed and breakfast until the investigation is complete and I can clear up.

I pack a bag of all I require for a week or so. I tidy all Kim's bits and bobs into a cardboard box, apart from the mementos I need for later, which go in a clear plastic bag. All the pieces I have curated of Kim and Rob's will leave this flat with me, along with the various letters from dead relatives. Some are destined for one place; some are needed elsewhere.

I slide my Queen journal into a tote bag for safe-keeping. Then I leave to spend time with Mum at the home.

Lesley leads me along the corridor as usual, and I say hello to Rob's mum in the passing.

'Can you look after this bag for me, Mum?'

I pass her a taped up WH Smith bag. The journal and letters nestle safely in there. 'It's a gift for Bertie,' I add. 'But I don't want him to find it in my flat.' I don't explain any further, and Mum doesn't question it.

'Oh, that's lovely, hen,' is all she says when I hand her the bag.

Maybe she has heard we got together but not the subsequent fall out.

I never mention the fire. She smelt smoke on me before, so no doubt she assumes I always smell that way now. Hopefully, Mum will forget all about this interaction.

Afterwards, I proceed to the dump to throw away all the unrequired odds and ends from the cardboard box. Then, after taking the car back to my flat's car park, I make my way on a walk with my trusty backpack containing the clear plastic bag. I wait for Kim on her regular dog walk.

SEVENTY-SEVEN

RHIANNON

SHE COMES out of the house and saunters along The Lagoons path. It's quite open on the main path, but she turns into a shortcut in between the main path and another public path. I find it so easy to creep up on her, like she used to do to me. I must be breathing loudly, maybe because of the smoke inhalation, but the dog doesn't even hear me coming.

For a moment, I simply stare at her from behind, feeling the power she took from me over the years return to my body. Then, I make my final move. I put my hand over her mouth and drag her into the bushes.

All my hiking has made me fitter than her, so I drag her out of sight in no time. The surprise must have left her weak. For once, she is not in charge.

She makes muffled noises as I push her face-first into the ground. I sit on her back and rest my foot on the back of her neck, so she cannot lift it. Her muffled noises become higher-pitched as she tries to scream, her mouth full of dirt. Her arms flail, and I laugh inwardly, thinking she looks like she is trying to swim.

I pull the black-and-white checked scarf I saved out of the clear bag in the rucksack and thread it under her chin, pulling it tight around her neck. Her hands try to grip it, to release the pressure, but she loses that battle and tires.

I roll her onto her back, straddling her so I can watch her expression as I pull it tight again. She is red-faced, almost resigned to her fate now.

I make out her mouthing some words—something about 'fire' as she stares wide-eyed. I watch her eyes bulging and listen to her gurgling squeaking noises as they fade out. I watch all her movements deplete until any life in her departs and the quiet commotion is over.

I stay still, in case she is acting and will explode to life as soon as I loosen my grip. Killing feels easier than expected. Relaxing, I raise myself to stand for a moment, staring at her. She wears her scarf with an odd expression of defeat. Scooter barks once, but licks my foot when he recognises me. Looking up, I notice a solitary rook disturbing the calm. It flaps away from the scene of the near-silent strangling.

I stand there for a few minutes more, my hands on my hips, my thumbs pressed into the small of my back, gazing towards the sea, sucking in the salty air.

SEVENTY-EIGHT

RHIANNON

THE NEXT DAY, I report Kim to the police as the person I believed had tried to kill me in the fire. 'I saw her in the alley,' I say.

'Go on.'

'I saw her in the alley with a red petrol can on the night. I'm certain.'

'Why would she do that?' the police officer asks.

I pause, inhale, and tell them, 'I had an affair with her husband. I'm not proud. He told me about her violent behaviour. She's a husband-beater. I felt guilty about the affair and told him to go back to his wife. He's not long back there. He must have told her all about it.'

'How did he take it when you said it was over?'

'He was really upset.'

'And?'

'Said he wanted me, but he would have to go back and suffer her. I told him as she was still his wife, morally I couldn't continue with him. He asked if we could be together if she was out the way?'

'What do you think he meant by that?'

'I dunno. Maybe if they were divorced or something?' I said she was still in the picture, so that was irrelevant. 'He wouldn't have done it, by the way, if you are thinking that. He wouldn't have tried to kill me.'

'So, he told her about the affair, do you think?'

'He was scared of her. Maybe he thought he could place all the blame for the affair on me and save himself from getting beat up.'

'She had motive?'

I stall again. 'Yes, and not just that. She never liked me. I used to work with her. She was a bully the whole time I knew her.'

'Right. So you have history?'

'Yeah, and there's another thing I need to tell you. It sounds far-fetched, but it all came back to me today after I was in the smoky flat. I watched her years ago doing the same thing. I forgot, because I was only five years old the last time I saw her at a fire. I was there when she burned her house down back in 1976. It was a vague memory, but the smoke must have triggered the memory. I heard her dad, Alec, after he barged out of the house, say, 'Kimberly, what have you done?' I remember it all clearly now. I must have blocked it out. I remembered because of the way she held the petrol can that day. She had one with her on the night she nearly killed me. A red one she was holding in exactly the same way.'

'Okay,' says the police officer. She glances at the second officer with wide eyes.

'That's a lot to go on with,' the other officer comments.

'I know. It all came flooding back. Maybe I was traumatised.'

She stares at me, and then blinks. 'Well, we'll have to investigate this further.' She reads the statement back to me, and I sign it. 'If you remember anything else, please contact us.'

As I head out, I spot Rob entering the building. I stand dead still and let him reach the counter. I'm afraid to make a move.

'I'm here to report a missing person. My wife is missing. She hasn't been home all night.'

He spots me and nods a slow, stony-faced hello. I shake my head and stride towards the door.

I hear him say, 'Her name? Kim.'

One of the officers who had been speaking to me does a double-take.

'Have a seat,' replies the officer at the desk.

SEVENTY-NINE

RHIANNON

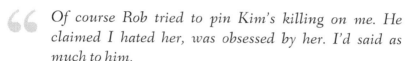 *Of course Rob tried to pin Kim's killing on me. He claimed I hated her, was obsessed by her. I'd said as much to him.*

He told them I'd possessed the murder weapon: the black-and-white checked scarf. He brought up the earring he found in my drawer, and that I had admitted I had broken into their house several times. But then, they only had his word for it.

I denied his claims. 'All ludicrous.'

The police searched my flat, of course, for the earring. They found nothing. It and any other items of theirs already resided in skip number ten at the dump. Jan identified the scarf as Kim's; she'd given it to her for Christmas.

'She cherished it and only used it for special occasions,' she said in the dock.

Not that much. She dropped it, and it ended up hanging on a lamppost.

'She would have never let it out of her sight,' Jan

carried on, 'and would have told me if it had gone missing.'

I hadn't furnished Rob with the details of how I got into their house. Even the police never picked up on the hatch in the fence. Post-murder, the dog magically appeared in the back garden via the famous hatch, my creative masterpiece. Scooter was my pal, of course, having stayed with me a few days. I placed him through the back fence without a sound. If the police had ever noticed the hatch, they might have imagined it was a fancy dog-flap.

Telling the police I believed Kim had tried to kill me days earlier gave me motive, but I made it appear as if I were the victim in all this, too. I had given up Rob, given up the affair to save his marriage, and I'd maintained this to the police beforehand. He appeared obsessed with me and wanted Kim out of the way.

In my testimony, I repeated I could not morally be with a married man due to what happened to me with Colin. Rob insisted he had walked out on me. It was his word against mine.

I gave a lovely performance in the dock, never letting anyone believe for a second that I could be the hurt party. He was every inch the spurned lover. Everyone knows rejection breeds obsession. Everyone wants to be the one who dumps the other. Better to be the dumper than the dumpee. When someone wants back with the one that rejected them, it's mainly to get them back by rejecting them in return.

I clench my teeth at the gall of him, choosing her over me every time. He deserved what he got.

I made sure the entire court thought he needed her out the way to live with me. I mentioned he seemed temperamental and quick to anger, and Jan and his work *mates backed me up. The most likely person to kill a woman is her spouse, so he topped their suspect list from the beginning.*

In my favour, Kim had behaved like an edgy bitch with many people. Her snide, catty remarks had not gone unnoticed. Even Sheona and Jan explained that, to an extent, when questioned.

I wonder where Sheona lives?

Then, of course, they brought up the sociopathic nature of her social climbing, her stealing the hockey club money. None of that painted her well. In contrast, I was clearly a 'people pleaser'. Most people considered me naive but nice. It seemed reasonable to believe she had bullied me.

Residue of petrol, courtesy of me, found on her coat implicated her in the arson. I had spied a red petrol can lying in their shed the time I'd hidden the remote control. Everyone happily believed she'd lit the fire at my flat. She didn't, of course. That was another of my performances, although I underestimated the damage. I needed it to appear realistic, but I'd taken it too far. I could have died.

The major evidence damning Rob was the button in Kim's left hand and the blue-grey fluff wrapped around her pinkie. Both matched a jumper in Rob's wardrobe. The random discovery of his odd boot near the murder scene, the pair for another in his wardrobe, was also a major find, although no one could explain why he hopped home after murdering his wife.

His hair under her fingernails, I thought was a lovely touch that showed signs of a struggle. Forensically, it was an open and shut case. None of my DNA was on her. Gloves and a mask, so commonplace these days, were a no-brainer.

What I did not realise until it was revealed during the trial was that Rob kept a journal detailing her abuse towards him. It might help him when they sentence him next week. Battered women get off with murdering their husbands, so perhaps a battered husband might expect some leniency.

To my benefit, it gave him even more motive to do away with her. It also detailed his obsession with me. His journal's last entry read: 'I have to put an end to all this.'

No, that's not right, the exact words were: 'I need to leave it all in the past, to deal with this once and for all.'

I remember the phrase and smile. Beautifully put, Robert.

It was a fabulous quote, thrown at him by the prosecution to gasps in the court and used in a number of headlines.

Everyone blamed Kim for the arson in 1976, since there was no one alive to contradict the theory.

I'd told the police about the earlier arson before the discovery of Kim's body, which tied in with her reason to bully me over all those years. I knew her secret; she must have always wanted me dead.

My return to the village had tipped Kim over the edge, brought out the arsonist in her all over again—that and the fact that I'd slept with her husband.

I was so much cleverer than silly Angela, slitting a man's throat in the flat and trying to hide a body in the bins. But I'd had practice.

EIGHTY

RHIANNON

Few people meet their great-great grannies, but I did. Granny Marie celebrated her ninety-sixth birthday in 1976, when I was five years old. I knew her fine.

I read the Hans Christian Anderson book she'd given me, The Little Match Girl, not understanding what the story was about. But I'd called myself that when I found the matches in the shed. Their smell appealed to me, as I stuck two together to produce a bigger flame.

I sat red-faced at Granny Marie's knee, by her immaculate fireplace, after Mother punished me for playing with the matches in the shed.

'Happy birthday to you,' I sang. Granny Marie lived in the house next door with Granny Irene. Marie, still active and sharp, seemed in her eighties rather than her nineties. She would still clean her step, the cleanest in the village.

'Did you get presents?' I asked.

'No, old ladies don't get presents.'

'That's sad.'

'Mummy said she caught you playing with matches.'

'Yes.'

'You aren't to play with matches. How did your wee fingers work that matchbox?'

'I did it like ...' I mimed the action. She chortled, and I realised I wasn't in for another telling off.

'Why has mummy said you are not to play with them?'

'The hut has a red can in it, and Mum said that could have gone up. Boom!'

'Here is a present you can get me. Go fetch that can and the matches, and I'll show you how to make things burn. You show me how you light the matches. Our secret.'

As she watched the fire, Kimberly had been holding a can—the one I'd dropped moments earlier. She'd picked it up off the ground.

I'd blocked it out for so long. You can't judge yourself a murderer at five years old and still function. The second fire brought it all into focus. I knew then what I was.

Still, I can't help but believe Granny Marie would have been proud of me today.

EPILOGUE

I VISIT THE OLD FOLKS' home to pick up the notebook with the Queen on the cover and all of the other journals and letters. I'm certain Mum never touched them or mentioned them to anyone.

Should I burn them all now? Or keep them?

I keep them.

I'm rushing to meet with Preston in Debbie's café. It has been two weeks since he was released from prison. Jan passed on his details last week.

'How was it, on the inside?' I ask.

'Terrible in a way, but I quite enjoyed the routine. The outfits were guff. The food was all right, cos guess who got to work their magic in the kitchen?' He spreads his arms out and points to himself.

'Brilliant.' I admire his ability to cope with any situation.

'Oh God, what about you, though? How was the whole trial business?'

'Hellish! The worst part was being interrogated as if I'd committed the murder. I felt as if I did it. Did that happen to you, too? Did they suspect you, make you feel like you'd done it?'

'Yeah, for a bit. But Angela confessed, so it was pretty much wrapped up.' He shrugs. 'I just said nothing, you know. No comment.'

'Must have been difficult for you.' I smirk.

'Yeah.' He takes a sip of tea, and when he spots me giggling, adds, 'Oh, shut yer face! How is the flat by the way?'

'Fine.'

'I don't think I could go back in there.'

'It's all sorted. You'd never realise anything happened in there.' I mean the fire, forgetting about the brutal murder he'd witnessed. I decide against explaining what I meant, as it does not seem to bother him.

'Did they really think you killed her at one point?' He turns the conversation back to the main point: Kim.

'Not really, but Rob insisted it was me. He tried to blame it on me.'

'No!'

'He had no alibi, plenty of motive, and all his forensics were at the scene.'

'Obviously him! What a nerve!' Preston taps his fingers on the table. 'As if!'

'Yeah—as if!' I pause. 'Man, I'd have hated to be convicted for something I didn't do.'

'Yeah, that would be terrible,' he replies, staring out the window, biting his lip. 'Terrible if the wrong person got the blame. Can you imagine?'

'I can,' I reply, following his gaze to the street, staring at—and feeling—nothing at all.

ABOUT THE AUTHOR

Emelle Adams live in East Lothian Scotland with her son and white cat.

https://twitter.com/AdamsEmelle

https://www.facebook.com/search/top?q=emelle%20adams%20-%20author

https://www.instagram.com/emelleadams1

The Bucket List

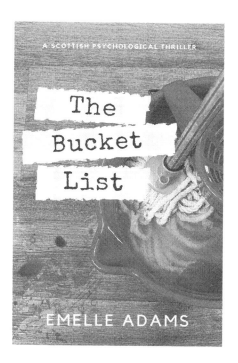

Angela is running out of time. Already 48 and terminally ill with brain cancer she starts a bucket list '50 things to do before 50'. But what she really wants to do before she kicks the bucket isn't 'walking with alpacas' or being an extra in a film or even finishing her memoirs. It is seeking revenge on all those who wronged her over the years, all those who definitely deserve to die before she does, all those who would otherwise get to see how the story ends, when Angela certainly won't ... or will she?

Printed in Great Britain
by Amazon

86426884R00180